Praise for

"I haven't read a book this great, this funny, this original, this emotional, this bonkers in quite some time. It's a little like Bukowski and Sam Lipsyte and the drug scene in *Beavis and Butthead Do America* all smashed together, but also completely and totally Kevin Maloney."

—Aaron Burch, author of *Backswing*

"*Cult of Loretta* is a hot dose of pleasure. It whistles with the wit of Brautigan, stings with the heart of badly dissolved romance. If a modern day mountain man came out of the wilderness with a story in his eye, this might be the thing he'd tell. Kevin Maloney is that kind of treasure—a wild thing that's come in from the war of life, lived to tell the tale."

—Brian Allen Carr, author of
The Last Horror Novel in the History of the World

"Kevin Maloney alchemizes the allure of dicey friendships, hallucinatory sex and a drug so terrifying I'm heartbroken I'll never get to try it. *Cult of Loretta* captures the manic fury of Richard Brautigan writing a sequel to *The Outsiders* during a ketamine binge."

—Jim Ruland, author *Forest of Fortune*

"*Cult of Loretta* is a book about a man named Nelson who gets his ass kicked over and over again by the world, and his heart pulverized over and over by the same enigmatic woman. It's about what happens to love when both halves of a couple are whacked out on the most powerful drug of all time. It's about the tragedies that parents can make for us, and the tragedies we make for ourselves. Kevin Maloney is an exceptional talent, someone capable of weaving all of these nasty little ingredients into something that is as tender as it is bleak, something that makes you laugh out loud as it rips open your skin and pulls out your veins."

—**Juliet Escoria**, author of *Black Cloud*

"Kevin Maloney drags the lake of our subconscious, revealing the often startling but always mesmerizing grit that becomes human memory. *Cult of Loretta* is an impressive debut, a confident showcase of an exciting new literary talent."

—**Michael J Seidlinger**, author of *The Fun We've Had*

CULT OF LORETTA

Joey,
So good to finally meet
in the flesh. Can't wait to
read your book!

[signature]

KEVIN MALONEY

LAZY FASCIST PRESS

LAZY FASCIST PRESS
PO Box 10065
Portland, OR 97296

www.lazyfascistpress.com

ISBN: 978-1-62105-183-1

For Tanna

CULT OF
LORETTA

Hang yourself, and you will regret it. Do not hang yourself, and you will also regret it. Hang yourself or do not hang yourself, you will regret it either way.

—Søren Kierkegaard, "Either/Or"

THE VICIOUS CYCLE OF SAMSĀRA

If Hoyt hadn't been a devout follower of Mahatma Gandhi's principle of non-violence, I would have died on the green carpet of my childhood bedroom with a heart around my neck inscribed with the name: Loretta Carter. But he was, so he never loaded his dad's gun, and when he pulled the trigger, the only liquid that shot out of me was piss—a dark blue circle growing around the fly of my jeans as I touched my face to make sure it didn't have a hole in it. He shook his head and said he'd never forgive me. Not if Hinduism was true and he had a thousand lifetimes to release himself from the vicious cycle of Samsāra.

That was the power of Loretta. The deeper you fell, the less you knew who you were. She made zombies of us. Addicts. Criminals. She dunked our heads in her fragrant water and pulled us up baptized. She made us men, and in the end, more than men. Broken adults searching for her face in our wives, always missing something, always remembering.

She was our Vietnam.

She was our forty days in the desert.

For a few years in the late 1990s, she was our god.

MISS MISERY

In 1998, Loretta watched Elliott Smith perform "Miss Misery" at the Oscars and thought it was the most beautiful thing she'd ever seen in her rotten excuse for a life. We lived in Aloha, Oregon at the time in a tiny bedroom in Loretta's grandma's trailer, about 17 miles from the house in Northeast Portland where Smith recorded *Either/Or*. I don't know if she'd been contemplating our escape for months or if she made her mind up right there on the spot, but when the song ended, Loretta turned to me and said she couldn't take it anymore; she needed to be closer to that pockmarked angel or to whatever sad perfect world made the man that made that music.

Two weeks later we moved into her cousin's basement in a dilapidated rental off NE Killingsworth. There were bars on the windows, mold in the walls, and something of a gang war raging on our block, but Loretta was happier than I'd ever seen her. It took her two days to find a job stripping at a club on Burnside. I was unemployed for six months sending out short stories to literary magazines.

One day I caught Loretta texting a customer she'd met at the club. She denied it and called me paranoid. Then she admitted she got high with him and let him go down on her in a Ford Mustang. She said she felt really bad about it but couldn't help it; she wasn't attracted to me anymore since I never had any money and didn't do anything all day but write stories nobody wanted to read.

I told her to go fuck herself and had a heart-to-heart with Dmitri, her cousin. He said, "Dude, let me tell you something about Loretta. She's a woman. Her body bleeds when the moon's full. They aren't like us, Nelson. For them it isn't about fucking; it's about money, stability, security. What are you trying to become again? A professional Nintendo player?"

"A writer."

"Yeah. Good luck with that."

He made a few calls and got me a job driving a forklift for a company that sold used medical equipment on Interstate Avenue, loading and unloading stainless steel IV poles, endoscopy obturators, arthroscopy pumps with hand controls. Things that rip people apart, put them back together, look inside and tell them when they're going to die.

When my supervisor handed me my first paycheck, I drove straight to Wells Fargo, cashed it, and threw the bills in Loretta's face, saying, "Do you love me now? Do you love me? How much money until you love me?"

THE BIRTHMARK, PART I

But first we were all in high school just trying to get laid. Loretta was a cheerleader. Her freckles should've made her ugly, but they made her impossible. They were all over her face: cheeks, jaw, forehead. They ran down her neck, but only on one side. She was a car wreck none of us could look away from. If the freckles did that to the face, what about her ass? Her pussy? What Jackson Pollock painting did God have in mind when he pushed that girl into the world?

Hoyt got to her first. Washing his hands with pink soap in the boy's bathroom one day, he announced, "Mystery solved, ladies. She doesn't have any on her tits. Just a birthmark. Bright red like her daddy poured boiling oil all over her on the day she was born."

I listened, imagining Hoyt as I've always imagined him—begging for his life with my heel kicking in his teeth. And loved Loretta even more.

RUDOLPH THE
RED-NOSED REINDEER

Who knows if she loved me or if she ever loved me or if she even thought about me with all those men sitting on barstools staring up at her birthmark that wasn't a birthmark, holding out dollar bills not quite far enough for her to take unless she discretely violated the "no touch" rule.

But I had a job—7 a.m. to 3:30 p.m., smoke break at 9, lunch at noon, another smoke break at 1:30—driving a 3-wheel pneumatic tire CAT that beeped when it backed up that I'd only twice backed into the metal frames of the storage shelves.

A 55-year-old African American woman named Sandy joined me on my smoke breaks. We sat on metal folding chairs and stared out at the rain, me in a torn Alice in Chains t-shirt, her in a low-cut blouse with a gold cross around her neck with a miniature gold Christ nailed to it that stared into the eyes of anyone who tried to stare at her tits.

We talked about a lot of things, but mostly I told her how miserable I was because my girlfriend was a stripper who had oral sex with her customers.

"Leave her," said Sandy. "Jesus Christ, Nelson. You're a baby. There's so much pussy out there. Eager pussy. Hungry pussy. Wet, juicy jungle pussy just dying to rub itself all over a handsome boy like you. What's so special about this Loretta?"

"Everything," I said.

"She sounds like a bitch."

It was fall, which chilled the air, crisped the maple leaves, and made love feel like something that would kill you if you weren't careful. Sandy wore a Rudolph the Red-Nosed Reindeer Christmas sweater and told dirty jokes through gold-capped teeth. I listened and laughed even when her jokes weren't funny. The sky was blue and empty with just a few contrails slowly widening, forming pale highways at 30,000 feet.

SITTING IN A BATHTUB WITH JEAN-PAUL SARTRE

Loretta and Hoyt dated for six months, but Hoyt was a prissy little bitch and everybody knew it. Eventually Loretta figured it out, and then he was just this gimpy boy following her around the hallways pretending he was her boyfriend, when everybody knew he was a boy pretending to be a man and she was a woman pretending to be in high school.

But before Loretta figured out how old she really was, she got super into Joy Division and the Dead Kennedys right around the time Nash and Tyson and I started our band. We didn't know three chords between us, but every day after school we hauled our gear over to Tyson's, ran extension cords out to his driveway, and performed for a small crowd of skaters who showed their approval by shaking their long hair and making the sign of the devil.

Nobody's dads were home from work and the moms tolerated us and made us sandwiches as Tyson bashed his drum kit spastically without paying attention to which song we were playing and Nash pushed his big red lips against the microphone and crooned the lyrics to songs I'd written but was too embarrassed to sing myself. Gems like: "A Dead

Jesus is an Honest Jesus," "Which Way to Nowhere?," and "Sitting in a Bathtub with Jean-Paul Sartre."

I played a sunburst Stratocaster, ripped off Jimi Hendrix chord progressions, and never looked at anyone, walking around with a tattered copy of *Thus Spoke Zarathustra* in my back pocket, growing my hair out as fast as possible.

ROSS

Loretta stripped five nights a week in Portland, then drove up to Seattle to strip at a different club on the weekends. She said it was the best way to get ahead in an industry that quickly tired of its dancers.

For the most part, I had the basement to myself. I jerked off imagining I was a famous writer, so famous my own girlfriend wanted to have sex with me. Then I'd read— usually biographies of great artists like Leo Tolstoy, Frida Kahlo, and John Coltrane. Sometimes I clunked the keys of a baby blue Smith Corona that Loretta bought me for my birthday, all covered in Nirvana and Dead Milkmen stickers. When I got stuck, I ransacked the apartment looking for proof of Loretta's infidelity.

I never found any, but one day I came across her bank statement with so many zeroes I thought I couldn't be reading it right.

"I'm going to college," she said the next time I saw her. "No loans. Then I'm going to buy a house."

She never said "we" anymore, but then again I didn't even know what "we" was.

One night she was in a bad mood and I asked, "What's wrong, baby?"

"My boyfriend's such an asshole," she said.

"I'm an asshole?"

"No. You're sweet."

Another night I came home and found her in bed watching *Friends*. I barely recognized her. She'd cut off all her hair and wore a fancy pair of underwear I'd never seen before. When I asked if we were ever going to make love again, she asked if I thought Ross was gay. "I always thought of him as, like, super gay. All that shit with Rachel—that was just because he was afraid to come out to Monica."

I told her that I liked Ross and thought he was the only one on the show who wasn't a complete asshole. And no, he wasn't gay.

She shrugged and we watched two more episodes together, and then she cried on my shoulder and said that Ken broke up with her.

"Who's Ken?" I asked.

"My boyfriend," she said.

"I thought I was your boyfriend."

"You know what I mean."

BLACKBIRD, PART I

Our high school had a courtyard full of gingko trees where you could pretend to be eating lunch but secretly get high on household solvents. It was Nash's turn to bring the drugs and he brought Comet. We took turns passing around that green cardboard tube full of powder, nobody quite courageous enough to shake some onto a history book and snort it up their nose.

"I heard this shit makes you see elves," said Nash.

"Where'd you hear that?" asked Hoyt.

"My cousin."

"Isn't your cousin dead?"

"Yeah, but he told me before he died."

What little sun shone down into that courtyard all seemed to fall on Loretta. She was sitting in the bark dust preparing for a Spanish quiz while Hoyt rubbed her feet and gave her hints regarding the conjugation of *ser*.

"Yo es stupido," said Loretta. "No puedo."

"*Soy*," said Hoyt. "Yo *soy* estúpida. Y sí se puede."

I sat in the shade away from all of them reading *Zarathustra* next to a girl wearing headgear.

Tyson sprinkled some Comet on the back of his hand and said, "Here goes nothing."

Everybody stopped what they were doing.

Zarathustra quit preaching.

The girl with the headgear looked up from *The Mists of Avalon.*

Hoyt and Nash couldn't seem to close their mouths.

"Tú es muerte," whispered Loretta, making the shape of the cross over her freckled collarbone.

Tyson looked up with blue powder flecked across his upper lip. "What?"

"Dude. You shouldn't have done that," said Nash.

"You brought it," said Hoyt. "What'd you expect? Tyson isn't afraid of anything."

Tyson seemed to be afraid of a lot. He stood up and started running across the courtyard and ran straight into the plate glass window of the library. A dozen honor students looked up from their SAT prep books.

We stood over Tyson, more or less watching him die, and then the school nurse arrived and then an ambulance.

When he came back to school a few weeks later, he was wearing a t-shirt with a black-and-white photograph of Sitting Bull on it. He said his name was Blackbird now, and after that, we called him Blackbird.

THE END OF THE WORLD

One day I got a letter in the mail. It was from Loretta, which was confusing because I thought she lived with me. It said:

Nelson,

I'm staying in Seattle for a while. Went to the UW campus to ask questions about scholarships, student loans, etc. & met a sociology professor named Bennie. He says the world's about to end, but when he sees me, he feels like everything's going to be okay. What I'm trying to say is—you should go out, meet people, fall in love. What we have isn't healthy. I'm not good for you. I'm more broken than you could possibly understand. Meet some sweet girl & make love to her & have babies. You're a good guy.

XOXO,

Loretta

I ripped the letter into confetti, then taped it back together and read it again. Then I put it in the toilet and pissed on it and took it out and dried it with Loretta's blow dryer. Then I folded it up and stuffed it in my back pocket and drove to Ray's Tavern.

Ray's was packed for the Blazers game, but I found a seat at the bar next to a middle-aged woman in a Public Enemy t-shirt. She smelled strongly of cigarettes and coughed like she had emphysema, but she reminded me of the Sears catalogue lingerie model I used to jack off to in middle school.

She asked if I thought the Trail Blazers were going to win. I said I was pretty sure they wouldn't because the world was a heaping pile of dog shit. She said, "Having a bad day?" I said, "My one true love wrote me a letter strongly encouraging me to have sex with other women."

She said that must be confusing and ordered me a drink called the "Three Wise Men," which consisted of a shot of Jim Beam, a shot of Jack Daniels, and a shot of Johnny Walker.

When the drink arrived, she said, "Don't get any ideas. Mercury's in retrograde."

I said, "I have no idea what you're talking about."

She said, "It means communication's a clusterfuck and neither of us should make any rash decisions."

"Okay," I said.

"My name's Stephanie," she said.

"Nelson."

We finished our drinks and went to her apartment and started groping each other on her futon. I was a little worried about Mercury, but Stephanie was all about rash decisions. She grabbed my hand and jammed it between her legs. It was a swamp down there. I moved my fingers around and

Stephanie made cooing sounds, but then I thought about the letter and wondered if this was Loretta's way of testing me and that if I passed we'd get married and have babies and raise them to be artists and scientists.

"What's wrong?" asked Stephanie.

Because I'd stopped moving my fingers, which gave this sex act a decidedly gynecological vibe.

"Nothing," I said.

I tried moving my fingers again, but when Stephanie moaned, I started crying. I said that I was sorry, but this was actually a test, which I'd almost failed but then passed at the last second. To prove it, I pulled Loretta's letter out of my pocket and read it to her.

She said, "It sounds like she's breaking up with you."

I said, "That's what I thought at first, but then I realized this is her crazy way of saying she loves me."

"I don't know," said Stephanie. "There's that part about her having sex with a college professor."

I'd forgotten about that part and became extremely depressed. Stephanie turned on the TV and we watched the local news and found out that the Blazers lost by 24 points and that some kid got hit by a car in Beaverton and died and that it was going to rain tomorrow and the next day and the day after that and would go on raining until a giant meteor hit the earth, which according to Loretta's new boyfriend was going to happen any day now.

$20 BILLS

We all graduated from high school, but nobody went to college because we were too busy doing drugs in the courtyard to study for our SATs. Also, our band was playing shows at La Luna, and other bands playing La Luna—like Heatmiser, whose lead singer was a 27-year-old named Elliott Smith—were getting signed and we all assumed we were about to get signed by Virgin or DGC or Capitol and be millionaires so bored with money that we burned $20 bills just to have something to do.

Hoyt was still in love with Loretta and thought he was dating her, but Loretta wasn't dating him, a miscommunication based on the fact that Loretta never actually broke up with him and still occasionally let him go down on her.

None of us suspected any of this, least of all that Hoyt was so strongly under the delusion that he was in a monogamous relationship with that freckled powerhouse, so when we finished our set and stood outside of La Luna on a Saturday night in 1996, the sky strangely clear and pockmarked with stars and barely-moving satellites, me in a torn black t-shirt, all sweat, Loretta in a tight-fitting Mudhoney shirt looking at me in a way I'd never seen Loretta look at me, I started talking to her.

We went to Dots and ate nachos, and then we drove back to her Gram's trailer in Aloha where she'd been staying since her mom kicked her out because she caught her huffing Pledge when she was supposed to be filling out college applications. Grams was asleep on the couch under an afghan, the TV turned to the Home Shopping Network. We tiptoed past glowing images of vegetable slicers to Loretta's bedroom, where we lay on top of the covers in our clothes listening to Iggy Pop on super low volume, talking about our childhoods, not kissing once until the sun rose pink through the blinds, and then we kissed like two eagles high in a canyon screaming over million-year-old rock formations.

I couldn't stop shaking and I accidentally came inside my underwear, but I didn't tell her, and as she reached to pull off her Mudhoney shirt, she whispered, "There's something I have to tell you about my chest."

THE BIRTHMARK, PART II

Hoyt wasn't far off, though when he said it, he was just being an asshole. Her dad hadn't pour boiling oil over her; her mom poured boiling soup on her because she was suffering from post-partum depression and Baby Loretta wouldn't stop crying. Obviously the soup didn't help, but it left a mark—a purplish-red stain roughly the shape of a manta ray that covered all of her left breast and most of her right. Hoyt was right about her freckles too. They stopped where the burn began, a meeting of skin catastrophes I found wildly exciting as I gently kissed her nipples and pretended that I still had an erection.

"Do you think it's gross?" she asked.

"Jesus, no," I whispered.

"You don't seem very excited."

"I'm *so* excited, I just—"

I was backed into a corner and the pink and orange colors of the sunrise were working their way up her legs, and I started to understand what I'd gotten myself into, thinking I was just eating nachos with the prettiest girl I'd ever met.

All I could think to do was lie and tell her I was a virgin, which she found sweet and assured me we'd take it slow. So we just held each other, listening to Iggy sing, "Everyone will be all right tonight," and for the first time in my life I thought Iggy was right, that the world was a big hunk of shit flying through space without meaning but a *good* hunk of shit, a hunk of shit where you could find a pretty girl and shake inside her arms on top of the covers listening to the wondrous sounds of rock and roll peppered with the clattering snore of a grandma in the other room.

COWBOY BOOTS

I hadn't heard from Loretta in weeks when she called asking me to FedEx her cowboy boots to Montana. Apparently Bennie was something of a world expert on the Y2K disaster and it was no joke, and while everybody else was partying like it was 1999, he intended to be living in a school bus in Helena, Montana on a piece of property he'd just bought, surviving on the milk of a small pack of Nubian goats.

Bennie asked Loretta if she'd like to leave her life of quiet desperation and join him. She said yes, but there was a super cute pair of black cowboy boots she'd left at her Grams's in Aloha, and would I be a dear and drive out there and ship them to her? She promised to pay me back one way or another, assuring me that even if she didn't, it would be good for my karma, a word I didn't think I'd hear Loretta use in a thousand years unless it was to mock the patchouli stink of the hippies on Hawthorne Blvd.

I told her to go fuck herself and her Y2K boyfriend. I said that as far as I was concerned, she and I were still dating.

She said, "Pretty please," and an hour later I was hugging her Grams.

Grams said, "Oh my goodness, have you grown? Can I make you a waffle?"

It was three o'clock in the afternoon, which seemed like a strange time for waffles, but I thought maybe this was my good karma coming back to me already, so I said, "Yes please," and a minute later we were sitting at a Formica table, eating Eggo waffles with Log Cabin syrup, watching *General Hospital* on a portable TV.

During the commercials, Grams asked how I was doing. I told her that I was deeply depressed and most likely an alcoholic. She gave me a kiss and said I was a hoot. Then she asked how Loretta was. I said that from what I understood, she was shacking up with a shady soothsayer who thought the world was about to end. She asked when I was going to do the right thing and ask Loretta to marry me.

We tracked down the black cowboy boots in the back of Loretta's closet, and while I was meditating on how all my misery started right there in that bed, I ran my hand along the top of her cabinet speakers and flaked off a big hunk of wax that smelled strongly of vanilla.

VANILLA

To be fair, I'd only had sex with two girls—Marla Nodelman and Lindsay Griffis—but those barely counted because Marla used a diaphragm and I couldn't feel anything, and Lindsay made me stop at two inches because she was Mormon and didn't want to go to hell and said it didn't count if it was just two inches.

Loretta wanted it to be special because she thought it was my first time, so we went to Bed Bath & Beyond and spent $100 on candles. I voted for unscented, but Loretta insisted on vanilla, and an hour later I was sitting on her bed in my boxer shorts watching her burn her thumb on the metal head of a cigarette lighter trying to get all those candles lit. We'd decided on Neil Young's *Harvest* as the soundtrack for my deflowering after briefly flirting with and rejecting the idea of using The Cure's *Disintegration* as being too depressing.

And so it is that I can't hear the song "Out on the Weekend" without seeing a skinny, 19-year-old version of Loretta standing in a yellow inferno of candlelight, the air claustrophobic with sweat and pheromones and vanilla, the windows already fogged up, Loretta swinging her hips to the sound of Neil Young's harmonica, too embarrassed to be entirely serious, but more serious than playful.

She wore blue underwear and a sleeveless Union Jack t-shirt, and all I wanted was for her to hurry up and get in bed with me so I could take off that shirt, but all I want now eighteen years later is for her to slow down, to take her sweet time, to never quite reach me. Because when she finally crawled up on the bed and took off her shirt and I kissed her scalded left breast and her half-scalded right one, it felt like the best thing that had ever happened to me, but it was nearly over.

I remember my hands shaking too bad to rip the condom wrapper and her reaching inside of my boxer shorts and gripping me and being so surprised that I coughed and she laughed and I kissed her open mouth and our teeth clicked.

I don't remember anything after that until I was lying on my back and realized that the third song on Neil Young's *Harvest* is "A Man Needs a Maid," which is pretty much the worst song ever. So that, even as I was falling off the cliff that is Loretta, noticing how happy she looked watching my face contort as I came for what she thought was the first time inside a condom inside a woman, Neil was playing the piano too loud, imploring the universe to send him a maid to clean up after him and do his laundry. There were bells ringing and violins, and Loretta asked if I'd mind if she skipped to the next song. I said, "Oh my God please," and she laughed and I laughed and I didn't feel anything until three years later when I hit the ground.

OUTSIDE

Outside Grams's trailer, I was contemplating throwing Loretta's cowboy boots in the dumpster, imagining one of those Nubian goats stomping her foot, breaking her big toe, her coming down with a Bob Marley case of gangrene and having that poor sweet nub amputated, but then I realized that white patch of scar where her toe used to be would be just one more fucked up part of Loretta to love. So I tossed the boots in the back seat of my Corolla and was about to drive away when a grown man stepped in front of my car, lowered himself into a three point stance, and said, "C'mon, Nelson. You still think you're hot shit? Let's see you get down here like a fucking man and go. On the count of six…"

BILLY, PART I

When I was in the sixth grade, my parents insisted that the best way to ensure I'd grow up to be an upstanding member of society was to play Pop Warner football. Pop Warner was basically an excuse for certain fathers who suspected that their sons might be gay to prove they weren't by commanding them to smash into each other as hard as they could and not die. More often than not, these dads, led by Coach Dan, forgot the ball at home, so we focused on tackling skills and "coming off the block," which was code for trying to murder each other.

I was pretty much a terrified mama's boy who'd just as soon be at home playing Nintendo, but I was six feet tall in the sixth grade, which looked vaguely intimidating to a gangly pack of five-footers whose dads thought they were homosexual.

Coach Dan blew his whistle and said, "Line up, ladies. Time for one-on-one. Dave, you go up on Carr. Nash, I want you on George. Nelson, let's try you with Timmy."

Like this they arranged us.

"On the count of six." Five. Four, three, two...

Timmy's three-point stance was all wrong. His butt was

high up in the air like he was trying and failing to touch his toes. The whistle blew and I exploded forward. Timmy didn't move. I smashed my padded shoulder into his unprotected chinstrap, and his bright lower teeth clipped his tongue, spraying flecks of blood through his braces. A flock of geese migrated across the pupils of his eyes.

Nine other collisions laid ten boys on the ground. They sat up and pulled clods of dirt from their facemasks. Toby Lynn said he couldn't breathe, but he always said that. The rest of us looked at each other with our hands on our hips, chewing the frayed plastic ends of our mouth guards.

In the end, it was me and Billy. Billy was fucked up in the head. I knew this on good evidence. He left sixth period every day to go to a counselor to talk about how fucked up he was. Everybody knew it, which made him uncommonly dangerous. He lived in a trailer and his dad was dead and supposedly he stuck it in a nineteen-year-old when they were both high on weed. The rest was in his eyes—blue like the lip of a torch, the tongue of a bird dying in the mouth of a fox.

He walked in concentric circles beating his fists against his chest. He'd settled into something. His calf muscles twitched in the rain and his face steamed. When he looked at me there wasn't any fear. There wasn't anything.

He took his three-point stance without anybody asking, and his legs were perfect little coils. I took mine and our eyes met. He licked his chapped upper lip. No gesture had ever scared me so much. The whistle was about to blow, but all I could think was, "You need to stop licking that lip, Billy. Put some Vaseline on it."

There was a sound, and for some reason I thought it was

a car horn in the parking lot. I understood a split second too late, and when the bells of our helmets collided, I saw his giant dry lip and dilated black pupils with nothing in them.

If his hatred was a well, I'd be at the bottom of it in an inch of water, shivering cold in a pile of dimes.

They pulled me up, but something was loose in my head. I hobbled over to the metal bleachers crying and swallowing. The sky went yellow with lightning and Coach blew his whistle. Billy jogged along next to him like he was a flake of light raining down from God's forge. He took off his helmet and his hair unwound in the rain and clung to his face. His eyes were the bluest things I'd ever seen. I'd give a thousand dollars to meet a woman with eyes like that.

He gave us our assignments, made sure we all had a ride to the game Saturday, then called practice. Kids got up and ran to the headlights in the parking lot. I laid my head back and my eye sockets filled up with rain.

"I had five dollars on you," said Coach. "Jesus Christ, he hit you. Neither of you flinched, but he caught you. I've never seen a harder hit in Pop Warner. That much force, the one who hits a little less hard takes it all. You got it, Nelson. You got it all."

BILLY, PART II

Billy stood up from his three-point stance, approached the driver's side of my Corolla, and socked me on the arm. He said he was fucking with me. He asked if I wanted to come inside and have a drink, catch up on old times.

I didn't want to be anywhere near that purebred wonder of hatred who'd nearly murdered me ten years ago, but I was thirsty and knew I'd start sobbing if I didn't drink something right away.

Inside, Billy's mother was sitting on the sofa, smoking a cigarette, watching *Oprah*. From the thick blue cloud, it seemed like she'd been chain smoking since the day she was born.

"Remember Nelson?" asked Billy.

She looked into my eyes, but she was drunk or she couldn't remember or she didn't care.

"I used to knock the shit out of him in Pop Warner. One time I hit him so hard he had to go to the proctologist to have his asshole sewn back together."

"Actually that was Toby," I said.

"Shit, you're right. Wait, what did I do to you?"

"You gave me a concussion."

"I gave everybody a concussion."

We went to his room and drank Johnny Walker. He told me his life story. He said he dropped out of high school back in '95 and joined the military. It was pretty fun, he said, smashing queers, learning about knives and whatnot, but then they shipped his ass to Kosovo where an anti-tank landmine exploded beneath the Humvee he was driving and something bad happened inside his brain.

They called it a "mild traumatic brain injury," but that was just because the VA was afraid to call it what it really was—hearing high-pitched screaming noises every second of his life.

"I can hear them right now," he said. "Like some invisible surgeon's drilling a hole through my skull."

"Right here," he said, pointing.

BILLY, PART III

Billy seemed to have a drinking problem too. He suggested we take a ride to the liquor store on his motorcycle. The liquor store was closed and we realized it was Sunday, so we went to the supermarket and bought beer. Billy said he kept a stack of dirty magazines hidden in the hollow of a tree in the forest near here, and did I want to go look at them? I said that sounded incredible.

Mostly they were *Hustler*s and one called *Barely Legal* and another called *Manga Burikko* that I'd never heard of before that Billy said was full of drawings of big-eyed girls done by perverted Japanese cartoonists.

We smoked pot and looked at all the magazines, and Billy said, "I don't mean this to sound weird, but I'm super turned on by photographs of black men dressed up as slaves pretending to rape their master's white daughter."

I told him that didn't sound weird at all, and he pried apart two pages of a particular *Hustler* to show me what he was talking about.

I don't know how the subject of Loretta came up, but when it did, he said, "Loretta Carter?" Then he made a V with his fingers, stuck his tongue through it, and flicked it up and down.

"My God, Loretta Carter. What a powerhouse. What a woman pretending to be a 12-year-old girl."

I asked him what he was talking about. He said he'd lost his viriginity to Loretta when they were twelve. I told him that wasn't possible because she'd lost her virginity to my buddy Hoyt who almost shot me.

"Is that what she told you?" he snickered.

He took another hit off his glass pipe, handed it to me, and said that in the strict sense, Loretta lost her virginity to her father, but it doesn't count if your dad rapes you in your sleep when you're nine. After that she lost her virginity to her brother Steve, but that didn't count either.

"Loretta has a brother?" I asked.

"He's dead, so technically no."

Billy said that eventually Loretta's mom figured out what was going on and got Loretta out of the house, but she had a pretty serious barbiturate problem, so Loretta went to live with her Grams in a trailer not too far from where he got down in front of my car in a three-point stance about an hour ago. That's where they met.

"We always heard you were having sex with some 19-year-old," I said.

"Ha. No, it was Loretta. She was 12 but everybody thought she was 19. She looked it."

He said he wanted to marry her even though they were still kids, but then he found out she was sleeping with Mr. Hennessy, the P.E. teacher.

"She had sex with Mr. Hennessy?"

"Oh yeah sure. He left his wife and they moved to Arizona for a while. It was a big hubbub. Her Grams told the police and they tracked them down and Mr. Hennessy served thirteen months in jail. That's why we ended up with Mrs. Ponteri taking over in the eighth grade, remember?"

He rolled up his sleeve to show me the scars on his arm from all the times he'd tried to kill himself while Loretta was in Arizona. The way they'd healed, they looked like earthworms.

BILLY, PART IV

We rode back to Billy's mom's trailer on his motorcycle and Billy asked if I wanted to shoot heroin and I said sure. We stuck needles in our veins and draped our heads backwards over the railing of his bed. The porno centerfold on his wall humped us so many times we curled up into balls. At one point I woke up and Billy was leaning over me, and for a second, I thought he was about to enter me like he'd entered Loretta in this same bed almost a decade ago. His eyes looked the way the sky must look when you're dying.

"Stay with me Nelson," he said. "You look funny."

He slapped my face and pulled down on my lower eyelids. He had a gap between his front teeth. I imagined pushing nickels through there, filling Billy up with money.

The next morning, Billy's mom came in holding two cups of coffee and found us on the floor next to her son's bed holding each other.

"You two," she said. "You're like babies. You look exactly like babies."

CAPOEIRA

When I got home from Billy's, Loretta's cousin Dmitri was practicing Capoeira in the living room to the frantic rhythm of berimbau music blasting from a 1980s-era boombox. I waved and Dmitri waved, then stopped mid-ginga, turned down the volume, and said, "Dude, we need to talk."

I pulled up a stool and he sat down next to me, shirtless, his long black hair tied in a ponytail.

"You need to come train with me," he said.

"Doing that?" I asked, pointing to the gym mat in the living room.

"Capoeira, man. This shit. It changes you."

"I'm fine," I said, my veins still sore from shooting heroin all night.

"You're an alcoholic," he said.

"I'm having a hard time," I said.

He told me all about the history of Capoeira. How it was invented by black slaves in Brazil in order to practice self-defense under the guise of dancing.

I thought of the photographs Billy showed me of those slaves having sex with their master's white daughter, in particular the girth of the slave on the left, how inadequate he made me feel, wondering how Loretta would ever be satisfied with what I had if there were guys walking around with pricks like that in their pants.

I thanked Dmitri for his advice but said I wasn't interested.

He said, "You know my cousin's having sex with some guy in Montana, right?"

I said I was aware of that fact and that it may or may not have something to do with my depression.

He told me that Capoeira was the perfect cure for depression, but when I buried my head in my hands and started sobbing, I must have looked like one sad bastard because he gave up on his sales pitch and held me and said, "It's okay, bud. We've all been there. But there's one thing I know—the sooner you let go, the sooner you'll start feeling better."

I went down to the basement and Dmitri's boombox turned back on, and for thirty minutes I lay on my bed thinking what a strange world this was that a Russian would spend hours alone in his house practicing the dance moves of Africans marooned in Brazil who were secretly plotting their revenge against millionaires who beat them to death to ensure the vigor of sugar plantations that produced a sweet crystalline powder rendered into lollipops to stick in the mouths of fat little babies to keep them from crying.

Then I wrote Loretta a letter. It went like this:

Dear Loretta,

I don't love you anymore. That's not true. I love you so fucking much. Why are you in Montana? I mean, is Bennie your true love? If so, then fucking hell okay. But if you're just running away from something, then maybe turn around and start running toward me? Or at least toward your daughter. When's the last time you even saw Allie? Your Grams asked about her and I didn't know what to say because I don't even know what she looks like anymore or if she's even alive.

Anyhow, I'm pretty sure I'm an alcoholic. Last night I shot heroin for the first time. It was pretty interesting.

What I'm trying to say is—I'm done with this life. Fuck it all. It was good knowing you Loretta.

—Nelson

WHAT YEAR IS IT?

Three days later, I came home from work and found Loretta sitting on the sofa in tears. She was wearing hemp jewelry, a patchwork dress, and smelled powerfully of goats.

"You fucking asshole!" she said, waving the letter in my face. "I thought you were dead."

I asked her what the hell she was talking about.

"Your letter," she said. "I thought it was a suicide note."

She read it back to me. She was right. It *did* sound like a suicide note. I wondered if I secretly wanted to die. Then I thought, *Wait, of course I do.*

Loretta said I wasn't allowed to pull this shit anymore. She was trying to build a new life in Montana with Bennie. She wanted to get her shit together, for real this time, and she didn't appreciate that preachy bullshit about Allie. What right did I have telling her what to do since apparently I thought it was a good idea shooting my veins full of heroin?

I started crying because she was right. I sobbed into my hands, and then I was almost knocked out by the smell of patchouli because, for the first time in I don't know how many months, Loretta's arms were wrapped around me.

I told her that I was confused because I still considered

her my girlfriend. I said that I loved her even though all the evidence suggested she was a sadistic serial monogamist. I told her that Dmitri tried to convince me to join his Capoeira studio, and for a few seconds, I actually considered it.

She rocked me in her arms and said things like, *There there* and *I love you baby*, which I didn't believe one bit, but then she took off her patchwork dress and we made love on the floor and it was the best sex we'd ever had because she was cheating on the man she was cheating on me with.

As she lay next to me on the scratchy gray fiber of the dirty carpet, smoking a cigarette, I started to understand why people cheat on each other. I didn't forgive Loretta for what she'd done, but I respected it.

The boombox came on upstairs and we heard the soft pounding of her cousin killing invisible slave owners.

Loretta said, "You need to get out of this basement. It's depressing the hell out of me, and I've only been here two hours."

Then she told me about the sky in Montana. She said, "Imagine looking out your window and seeing three different states and clouds so big they could kill you without even trying."

I listened thinking of Billy's eyes.

She said what I needed was to come out to Helena with her and breathe a little. Spend some time on the farm with her and her boyfriend.

I asked her why she kept sleeping with me if I wasn't her boyfriend.

She pinched one of my testicles and asked me what year I thought this was.

THE GOAT FARM

We drove from Portland to Helena in Bennie's 1964 Ford pickup, taking turns pissing in a Gatorade bottle, Loretta using a funnel rigged for the purpose. The green trees of Oregon gave way to yellow grass, high desert, and a sky like somebody cut off our eyelids.

Bennie's Goat Farm was a one-acre parcel of a 100-acre lot partitioned with barbwire, distinguished by a rusted-out school bus, the strong stench of goat farts, and a hand-painted sign that read:

THE END IS NEAR
DON'T REPENT
GET YER SHIT TOGETHER!!!

When Bennie saw the pillar of dust rising from the tires of his Ford, he stepped out of the school bus to greet us with two frothy mugs of still-warm goat's milk.

"Loretta, my often-drunk beauty queen!" he screamed.

"Bennie, my slightly-paranoid goatherd!" she replied.

She didn't even have the cab door halfway open and he'd already lifted her in the air and was swirling her around by the armpits.

He looked pretty much the way I'd pictured him—six-foot-seven, bald, with an epic Grizzly Adams beard. But I hadn't expected him to be entombed in a neon yellow HazMat suit.

He took off his helmet, gave Loretta a kiss, and said he didn't think she was serious about bringing me back to Montana.

She said, "You never believe anything I say. You think I'm a rich bitch from the suburbs."

"Aren't you?" he asked.

Loretta introduced us and Bennie said, "The other boyfriend! My God, it's *so* good to meet you!"

He gave me a bear hug and said that if I was up for it, he'd like to eat psychedelic mushrooms with me and talk about the universe.

We walked around the farm drinking milk that tasted like somebody's scrotum while Bennie described at scientific length why Nubians are a superior breed of goat, not even close by a mile.

When he turned around to point out a particular goat named Rebecca who had an inexplicable but fully operational extra utter, Loretta pointed a finger at her temple and made a swirling motion to indicate that the man she was cheating on me with was completely out of his mind.

It was 6 p.m. and Loretta said she was starving. She suggested we knead up some sourdough for a pizza crust and fire up one of their goat cheese beauties in the wood fire oven.

Bennie reminded her that there was a rave tonight at the quarry starting at 8 p.m. and they might not have time to make pizza *and* enjoy a "welcome home" round of lovemaking.

Loretta said, "Oh dang, I totally forgot about the rave," and started taking off her clothes.

44

BANG

Actually, one of us was going to college. Hoyt secretly enrolled at PSU and signed up for three courses including *PHL 222: Thoreau, Gandhi, and King: The Politics of Right Action.*

While Loretta and I spent that September exploring each others' bodies, telling each other what we liked and didn't like, experiencing mysterious forms of intimacy (like the time my condom came off inside of her while she was rubbing against me after I came and we realized that her vagina was full of my semen and that she might have a baby and that I'd have to stick my fingers in there and find the condom and pull it out—which I did), Hoyt was learning about the Salt March, Gandhi's spinning wheel, and starvation as a weapon of civil disobedience.

I'm still not sure what he knew and how much and when, but Loretta and I had been dating almost three months when I came home from my part-time job at the record store, walked upstairs to my bedroom, felt a hard thud at the base of my skull, and promptly fell to the ground.

When I came to and rolled onto my back, Hoyt pushed the nose of his dad's Sig Sauer an inch deep in my mouth.

"Sorry," he said. "About hitting you."

I couldn't say anything since I had a gun in my mouth, so I decided to listen.

"Is it true?" he asked. "About you and Loretta. Are you fucking my girlfriend?"

I nodded. How could I lie? Everybody knew, and I seemed to be wearing a necklace she'd made with her name and my name inscribed inside an anatomically correct heart.

"You fucking ratdick," he said.

I wouldn't have known what to say even if I didn't have a gun in my mouth.

"She's my fucking woman, man. My girl."

He was crying. Also, he was extremely skinny. Only much later did I learn that he'd been protesting our relationship by not eating ever since Blackbird mentioned that I never showed up to band practice anymore now that I was dating Loretta.

If I'd known there weren't any bullets in the gun, I would've calmly removed the barrel from my mouth since Hoyt seemed too weak to pull the trigger. But I didn't know that, and if he wasn't, I wouldn't get a second chance at anything for all of eternity.

Finally he sighed and said, "Goodbye, Nelson," and pulled the trigger and the gun went *click* and I pissed myself and Hoyt said, "Bang," and it was the saddest word I ever heard in my entire life.

THE FUCK YOU NELSONS

I don't know if it was the taste of Hoyt's dad's gun or contemplating the possibility that the afterlife would be as boring and forever-seeming as the beforelife, but some time around then, late '96 or early '97, I sank into a deep depression that rendered me a lackadaisical and entirely unreliable guitarist. During the middle of performances I tended to do things like play songs in the wrong key or hold my guitar like a baby and kiss the tuning pegs or grab the microphone from Nash and yell at the audience: "Tell me anything matters. Prove to me that anything matters!"

Nash seemed to think my antics were affecting our chances of getting signed by Virgin or DGC or Capitol and becoming millionaires so bored with money that we burned $20 bills just to have something to do.

One day I showed up to band practice and a kid named Adam was strumming a Gibson Les Paul, standing on the oil stain on the garage floor where I usually stood. There was a young woman next to him holding a tambourine who, I realized, was the same girl with the headgear who used to sit in the courtyard reading fantasy novels back in high school.

Nash informed me that he'd decided to shake things up

a little. The band had a new guitarist, a new percussionist, and a new name: Nash Derbes and the Fuck You Nelsons. He said he didn't see a place in the new lineup for a guitarist who thought it was funny and/or interesting to tune his guitar during the middle of a solo.

I said, "That's sort of funny because none of this even exists."

He said, "So we're good then?"

I said, "Jesus Christ. We're fucking great!"

I hit the button on the garage door opener and stepped outside and watched a crow fly across the blue sky and knew that my soul was a single molecule of H_2O falling over the precipice of Niagara Falls and that life was giant and mysterious and most likely meaningless. I took the bus downtown and bought a black-and-white Mead composition notebook and a small package of pens and attempted to write a philosophical treatise about the fleeting nature of existence, only to find that I'd drawn a picture of a skull with infinity symbols for eyes and that I was more afraid of death than ever.

ZEN AND THE ART OF DEATH

I did a little research on the art of staying calm in the face of unavoidable, permanent death and found out about a Zen center in Northwest Portland where, according to the flyer, men and women achieved inner peace by contemplating thousand-year-old jokes about rivers and butterflies. Wednesday night was Open Sit so I decided to give it a shot.

When I arrived, the entryway was filled with people in dark clothes speaking in quiet voices about "the dharma" and a retreat that was happening that weekend—would there be snacks, and if so who was bringing them? Not Dale, right? A few people gave me strange looks that I attributed to my Primus shirt, which showed a bulging-eyed pig drowning above the words "PORK SODA."

A gong rang and we walked into another room and sat on blue cushions facing a calligraphic circle. A woman in a black robe hit the gong again, and immediately it became clear that the next hour of my life was going to be extremely boring. The only sounds were the building's heating unit and the occasional car driving by and the cough or fart of one of my fellow meditators.

I tried to clear my head of all thoughts and replace them with serene images like unicorns and waterfalls, but my mind was fickle and sickly and one of the unicorns grew a cancerous tumor and died and I watched its white carcass ripped apart by opportunistic scavengers and satanic insects.

The gong rang again and I thought, *Thank fucking God*, but we were still meditating, only now we were walking in a circle and I couldn't feel my left leg and every time the guy in front of me took a step, his knee clicked and I thought about bones and how everything falls apart.

By the time it was over, I was pretty sure I'd lost my mind. The Zen priest, a woman named Carol, came over and asked if it was my first time at the Dharma Center. I said that it was. She asked me what brought me here. I said that I was feeling bummed and panicky about the fact that I was going to die one day. She said that meditation was a wonderful way to address anxiety issues.

I said, "Anxiety isn't my issue. It seems like an entirely appropriate response to my impending death."

"You're sick?" she asked.

"Oh God," I said. "Probably. It hurts everywhere."

She handed me a book called *Zen Mind, Beginner's Mind* by Shunryu Suzuki and encouraged me to read it and follow the path of satori.

I took her advice and read the book in the bathtub of Loretta's grandma's trailer. According to Suzuki, enlightenment isn't answering the big questions like, *Why am I here?* and *What happens when I die?* but is simply a matter of having good posture and breathing right when you meditate. God, what a horrible joke! The point of existence was basically what my mom had been strongly encouraging me to do at the dinner table since the day I was born.

I started crying, but then Loretta came into the bathroom and peed sitting next to me, and I listened to the sound of her tinkle hitting the toilet water and thought, *At least there's this. What beautiful music!*

SPEAKING OF MUSIC

Speaking of music, a few days later Loretta said that Nash Derbes and the Fuck You Nelsons were playing a show at La Luna and would I be her date? I told her that it felt sort of weird going to the show of a band whose name was an aggressive insult directed explicitly at me. She said, "Don't be such a sourpuss," and a few hours later we were getting elbowed in the ribs in the mosh pit of a sold-out show where Nash sang songs from his new album. Gems like: "A Best Friend is a Dead Friend," "Which Way to Nelson's Tiny Dick?," and "Sitting in a Bathtub with Loretta Carter."

The last of these songs was an extremely pornographic power ballad.

I grabbed Loretta by the arm and said, "This is bullshit. Let's get out of here."

She said, "Have you ever noticed Nash's eyes? They're like Amazonian tree frogs."

I said, "That's kind of funny because Nash's eyes don't even exist."

She said, "I just want to hear the rest of this song."

While I practiced a form of voodoo that involved jabbing my own hand with a Bic pen, Loretta took off her bra and threw it on stage. Then Nash took off his shirt and wrapped her bra around his neck like a boa and mouthed the words, "I want to fuck you so bad," and the band broke into a cover of The Doors' "Light My Fire" and Nash invited Loretta up on stage and I said, "Fuck this!" and stormed outside.

It was pouring rain and my hand was bleeding and the meaning of life was having really good posture.

I sat on the ground and cried and jammed my pen into my thigh until the bouncer came over and said that what I was doing was pretty punk rock, but kind of gross and did I mind doing it somewhere other than the entrance to La Luna?

I walked around the city soaking wet, giving away all my possessions to homeless people, including: 1) a bloody pen, 2) *Zen Mind, Beginner's Mind* by Shunryu Suzuki, and 3) 76 cents.

Then I sat on a park bench and took stock of my life. From the look of things, I was the new Hoyt, though I had no intention of shooting anyone or starving to death or pretending that Loretta and I were still dating.

I decided to kill myself.

Fuck it.

Then I realized that after the glorious FUCK YOU that would be my self-inflicted death, I would be dead and therefore unable to enjoy it or anything else for all of eternity, so I decided to come up with a better idea.

THE RAVE, PART I

We arrived at the rave at 8 p.m. sharp, but the quarry was deserted.

"Guess we should have made pizza," said Loretta.

"These things take time, honey bun. Be patient," said Bennie.

We parked on a ridge overlooking the valley. It was cold, so the three of us snuggled up together under a blanket. Bennie loaded a two-foot bong and we each took a hit and held it in too long and coughed like we had bronchitis.

A thousand bats circled overhead, black half-realities shooting briefly across the indigo. Bennie said, "Man this rave is wild."

Loretta took turns kissing us, and then we took GHB, a liquid date rape drug that felt like semen rolling around on our tongues.

Bennie said, "You guys, you can totally see the Milky Way from here."

We looked up and saw a purple watercolor bleeding over the stars. It reminded me of how tiny and ridiculous my body was in the grand scheme of things and that it didn't really matter if I was alive or dead.

The bats gave way to coyotes, then the voices of ghosts.

I asked Bennie, "Why the HazMat suit?"

He said, "We're on a nuclear reservation."

"Then why do you live here?" I asked.

"Cheap," he said.

They weren't ghosts. They were Montanan teenagers high on drugs. They found our pickup.

They were the opposite of us—two girls and a boy. The girls had dreadlocks. The boy had bloody scratch marks up and down his arms and was missing both front teeth.

"Bike accident," he whistled, straddling a Huffy in a tank top that said "EAT MY SHIT" in black Sharpie.

We got them high, and then Loretta started kissing the kid on the bike. His name was Eric. He put his hand down the front of her shorts and licked the outside of her mouth. He said, "Dang you're weird looking." Loretta said thanks and they went off together to find gemstones.

Bennie and I stayed behind and drank beer with the hippie girls. One of them said her name was Yesterday. She pointed at the Big Dipper and said it looked like a pot pipe. Then she told us that when she was five, her dad was up in a bucket truck trying to fix a power line when a school bus plowed into him; he fell thirty feet and smashed his brains on the blacktop in front of 37 second graders.

The other girl listened, making hemp jewelry. Bennie kept saying, "Heavy. Heavy, man. Heavy."

I got worried about Loretta and went looking for her. Soon we were all looking, wandering around the quarry. Somebody turned on a flashlight, and then we saw incredible things, like shale and veins and rainbow-pierced quartz inside of glowing yellow circles.

We found Loretta and Eric by a campfire, naked inside an Oakland Raiders blanket. Two-thirds of Loretta's manta ray was visible. I couldn't tell if they'd just made love or if the goat smell was Loretta's little burps regurgitating her glass of body-temperature milk.

I started crying because I realized that Loretta wasn't a sadistic serial monogamist, she was a nymphomaniac. But the longer I looked at her, the more I realized it wasn't Loretta. She had Loretta's face and body, but there was dust under one of her nostrils and one of her eyes was crossed. She'd just done screw for the first time. She was in the Other Country.

THE RAVE, PART II

Something like a four-armed elephant god seemed to be revealing itself to Loretta with the soft touch of a serial killer sawing the arms and legs off a prostitute. I'd never seen her look so stunned and simultaneously in wonder of it all.

Eric was holding an imaginary AK-47, pointing it at each of us, going, *Atta-atta-atta-atta. Got yer skull and yer skull and yer skull and yer skull!*

Loretta held up her hand and said, "It's bones. After everything they taught us, we're just goddamn bones!"

This rave was getting out of hand. I grabbed Loretta and said it was time to go.

She said, "What happened to your skin, Nelson? You look like a pirate flag."

I said that from what I could tell, she'd ingested a drug stronger than Comet and that I didn't care which of us was her boyfriend, somebody had to take control of the situation.

Bennie said, "Oh dang, they're screwheads."

I asked, "What's a screwhead?"

He said, "Everything's bigger in Montana."

Loretta said, "I'm not going anywhere; I just crawled inside my mother."

Bennie said, "Settle down Nelson. This is a rave. When in Rome."

Eric cut Bennie a line. Bennie snorted it, looked up, and said, "Jesus, Nelson, what happened to your skin?"

I didn't want anything to do with screw, but one of the hippie girls started kissing me and I kissed her back, not realizing she'd just rubbed screw into her gums.

First there is a black lake.

Then you die.

Once you're dead, you go inside your mother again.

This is called the Other Country.

Here they remove your skin. At this stage you're called a "poltergeist."

Kissing the hippie girl, I could see her bones. I couldn't remember her name and she used too much tongue, but her eye sockets were wonderful.

I thought of Mrs. Adams's art class, the day she opened the broom closet, brought out a skull, and said, "It's time to draw heads." She put it on a pedestal in the middle of the room and everybody got out their notepads. I started to draw, but the whole time I kept thinking, *Jesus—whose face used to be attached to that thing?*

THE RAVE, PART III

For a while we were skeletons. Then my mom showed up.

I said, "Jesus Christ, Mom, what are you doing in Montana?"

She said, "Are you high on drugs, Nelson?"

I told her that I was and that I was really sorry for all the stupid things I'd done in my life, in particular using drugs and not going to college.

She just shook her head, took off her pants, pulled down her underwear, and I crawled inside her vagina.

It was red in there and black and kind of gummy, and it smelled like when you leave a packet of Thousand Island dressing in your car overnight.

I said, "Can anybody see anything?"

Loretta and Eric and Bennie and the two hippie girls said, "No. We're all inside our mothers' vaginas."

For a long time we were quiet, experiencing weightlessness, hearing the immense songs of orcas swimming around imaginary archipelagos. It was pretty much the best feeling of my entire life. Then I used up all the serotonin in my brain and couldn't experience joy anymore. The whole world turned dark and ugly, and I was a piece of shit in a black valley called NO WORDS.

I said, "Does anybody else feel like everything's shit?"

Somebody said, "Oh god oh god it hurts."

Then I saw Immanuel Kant riding a bicycle, and I was like, "What the hell, Immanuel Kant? What are you doing here?"

He said, "Shhhhhh!" and I remembered the name of the valley.

An hour later we sobered up and found ourselves lying on our backs, swirling our legs in the air like we were riding imaginary bicycles.

"This is why I renounced cars for Huffys," said Eric, scratching his arms.

Nobody yanked their veins out that night, but a few of us tried.

Eric had to get stitches.

Loretta finally pulled out her front tooth.

Bennie took off the HazMat suit and said it didn't matter anymore. Everything was tearing him apart.

WHAT HAPPENED TO NASH, PART I

I was under the impression that my girlfriend had fallen in love with my best friend because he'd sung a pornographic power ballad about making love to her in the sloshy water of a bathtub, but it didn't happen like that at all. Three days earlier, while I was sitting in the lotus position trying to clear my head of all thoughts and replace them with serene images like unicorns and waterfalls, Nash was knocking on Loretta's grandma's trailer, holding a demo he'd recorded on his four-track titled "The Yoko Ono Syndrome." He wanted to give it to me so I could hear how much better the band sounded now that it had a guitarist who believed in the existence of his guitar.

Loretta answered the door and said, "Dang, you just missed him."

Nash said, "You know what, woman, it's because of *you* I recorded this," waving the cassette angrily in the air.

He meant it in the meanest, most poisonous way, since it was on account of Loretta that Hoyt almost shot me, rendering me a lackadaisical, unreliable guitarist. But Loretta misunderstood and thought that Nash had recorded an album of original songs dedicated to her because he was in love with her.

She said, "Oh my God. That's so fucking sweet," and asked if he wanted to come into her bedroom and play the album on her stereo.

Nash was deeply confused, but Loretta was wearing Revlon "Love That Red" lipstick which made her lips look like a woman's genitals flooded with blood and had the effect of flooding Nash's genitals with blood. He cleared his throat and said "yes" so quietly that Loretta wasn't sure he'd actually spoken.

They sat on her bed listening to all six songs of Nash's demo, Nash sweating and apologizing for parts of the recording that hadn't come out right, Loretta assuring him that it was perfect just the way it was.

When it was over, Loretta said, "That's the most beautiful thing I've ever heard in my rotten excuse for a life."

Nash said, "Really?"

Loretta said yes and told him to strip down to his boxer shorts while she changed into something comfortable.

When she stepped out of the bathroom, she was wearing blue underwear and a sleeveless Union Jack t-shirt. She put on Neil Young's *Harvest*, lit 100 barely-used candles, and even though Nash had once traded a pack of cigarettes for a blowjob from his female coworker at Subway, he was still a virgin in the dick-in-vagina sense, but not anymore as Loretta wiggled out of her blue underwear, struggled trying to get a condom on him, gave up, and slipped Nash inside her deepest, wettest place without anything between them but fire.

Nash almost lost his mind. It felt so good he didn't

understand that he was still a human being. When he managed to gain something like consciousness, he noticed that Loretta was holding a remote control.

"Why are you holding a remote control?" he asked.

"No reason," she said, gyrating her hips.

"Slow down slow down I'm going to come," he said.

Neil Young sang, "Dream up, dream up, let me fill your cup with the promise of a man," the last line of the song "Harvest," but before he could launch into "A Man Needs a Maid," Loretta pressed skip on the remote control.

And so it was that Nash heard the opening chords of "Heart of Gold" as he came in three distinct jets inside of Loretta, and she smiled as she'd once smiled for me and Hoyt and 12-year-old Billy, but not for her father or her brother Steve.

WHAT HAPPENED TO NASH, PART II

Nash was in love. He was so in love that his mind became a beehive of crazy ideas—things he'd never dreamed he was capable of like showing up at a girl's trailer with a pot of bougainvillea to tell her how much he loved her and wanted to have babies with her and raise them to be productive members of society.

But when he knocked on the front door, Grams opened it and said, "Loretta? Take a number."

"What do you mean?" he asked.

"The other boy's in there," she said.

"Nelson?"

"Oh God," she said. "How many of you are there?"

Nash barged past Grams, flung open Loretta's bedroom door, and found the love of his life sitting on the Fuck You Nelsons' new guitarist's lap in a particularly acrobatic version of the reverse cowgirl. She wasn't wearing any underwear, but she had on a certain sleeveless Union Jack t-shirt and the room glowed with the light of 100 half-used candles and Neil Young was singing "Words (Between the Lines of Age)," which Nash knew was the tenth track on

Harvest. He did a little math and calculated Adam's stamina at 37 minutes and counting (33 if Loretta skipped "A Man Needs a Maid") and promptly lost his shit.

Adam said, "Slow down slow down I'm going to come."

Nash smashed the terracotta pot against the wall, picked up the sharpest, most menacing-looking shard, pressed it against Adam's jugular, and said, "If you come, I'll fucking kill you."

Loretta cried and said she loved them both and asked if anybody was interested in a threesome.

Nash accidentally quoted Hoyt, pleading, "She's my fucking woman, man. My girl."

Adam said, "Your woman? I thought she was Nelson's woman."

Nash made a lot of threats, and while he didn't believe in Gandhi's principle of non-violence, he didn't have the heart to murder his new guitarist (or the love of his life) with a piece of terracotta. Instead he decided to take his own Magellan-like voyage to Eternity to find out what all the hubbub was about.

THE SUICIDE NOTE

Dear Adam, Loretta, other traitors & friends of current/former incarnations of Nash Derbes & the Fuck You Nelsons,

I'm by no means on Nelson's side of things, but I think he's pretty close when he says that none of this exists. What I mean is, none of us knows what the fuck this is, this Mystery with a capital "M," the eye above the pyramid on the back of a dollar bill. Not me, not Adam, not Nelson, not Loretta, not Blackbird, not the girl with the headgear (sorry I don't know your name).

What I'm saying is, I'm tired of all this speculating. We're just monkeys throwing shit at the wall to see what sticks, but I want to know the TRUTH, see it with my own goddamn eyes.

So, until we meet again—I love you all!!!

XOXO Nash

P.S. Except Adam & Loretta. You two—eat shit and die.

WHAT HAPPENED TO NASH, PART III

He left the suicide note on the kitchen counter, accidentally quoted Blackbird, saying, "Here goes nothing," and jumped out the third-floor window of his apartment building.

When Blackbird and I went to visit him at St. Vincent's Hospital, he was lying on a gurney with tubes up his nose penning a treatise on the afterlife in the margins of the Holy Bible—proverbs of sorts, like his declaration in the crease between Corinthians 12 and 13: "There *is* a white light at the end of the tunnel, but it isn't your dead grandma in there. It's more like a Björk video: crags of ice, elfin magic, drum machines."

"Hey, man," I said.

He opened his mouth but only a gurgle came out.

"Sorry your face is fucked up," I said. "Does it hurt?"

He gave me the thumbs up, which either meant *doing fine* or *what do you think, fuckhead?*

I probably should have been pissed, since it was Nash's fault that I wasn't having sex with Loretta anymore, but seeing him in a hospital gown with an EKG hooked up to his heart, I decided to forgive him. I understood that we were all bastards, that any man with blood in his veins who had a chance to sleep with Loretta would take that chance and gladly be destroyed.

I handed him a card signed by his fellow bandmates, including the girl with the headgear whose name, it turned out, was Clementine.

Blackbird said, "I know what you're feeling right now, brother. Remember the time I snorted Comet and ran into that plate glass window? Well, I never told anybody this, but I had a near death experience; I saw a bright white light that I thought was a spaceship, but turned out to be ghosts who told me that I'm a quarter Cherokee."

Then he said he'd seen Adam's wang once and it was only about an eighth of an inch long, so technically Adam hadn't had sex with Loretta because that'd be like a wall trying to make love to a woman.

Nash tried to smile, but he didn't have any teeth and his jaw was full of wires.

WHAT HAPPENED TO NASH, PART IV

Failure only whetted his appetite. A few days after they let him out of the hospital, Nash called his brother Royce, a drug dealer up in Yakima, and asked if he could score his little brother a cocktail of barbiturates that would shoot him like an arrow into the bull's-eye of Jesus.

Royce drove down from Yakima and handed Nash a sack full of pills every color of the rainbow. When Nash dumped them onto the kitchen counter, they looked like Skittles.

Nash said, "So you're sure these'll kill me, bro?"

"Like the fuckin' plague," said Royce.

"So this is what Death looks like?"

"No," said Royce. "That's what pills look like."

Then Royce gave his brother this farewell message: "So I don't expect Dad'll be wherever it is you're going, but if he is, tell him he was wrong about my car. It was the serpentine belt."

Nash swallowed as many pills as he could fit into his mouth, washed them down with Powerade, thanked his brother for doing him this solid, and died.

WHAT HAPPENED TO NASH, PART V

The morgue at St. Vincent's Hospital found my name and phone number on the back of a set list they pulled out of Nash's jean pocket before they pushed his body into a 10,000-degree oven. They called and asked if I wanted his ashes.

"Doesn't his family want his ashes?" I asked.

"Have you ever met his brother?" they said.

I was expecting an urn, but their urns started at $49.99. I told them a cardboard box was fine.

I put Nash on the passenger seat of my Corolla and took him for a drive. I was feeling nostalgic, so I drove back to the Subway in Aloha where Nash used to work. Mercedes, his former co-worker who'd supposedly once traded him a blowjob for a pack of blue American Spirits, was standing behind the counter in a green visor, doing lines of cocaine off the cutting board where she made people sandwiches.

When she saw me, she said, "Jesus Christ, Nelson, how the hell are you?"

I said pretty bad and told her about Nash.

She started crying.

We went out back behind the Subway and shared a cigarette and told stories about Nash from back when he was alive. I told her about the time we did psychedelic mushrooms together and pretended we were old Japanese men who'd found enlightenment. She told me about the time she gave Nash head in exchange for cigarettes. She said that when his dick got hard it flipped up and touched his belly button and she could barely pry it away to get her mouth around it. Then she started sobbing and said she couldn't stand the thought of Nash's big red lips getting eaten by maggots.

I said that actually they put him in a 10,000-degree oven and that I had what was left of him in a box sitting on the passenger seat of my car. She didn't believe me, so I showed her.

We opened the box and there was a plastic bag inside sealed with a bread tie. I removed the tie and Mercedes ran her fingers through Nash and came across part of a tooth. She asked if she could have it. I said I didn't see why not.

Mercedes said she couldn't work under these conditions. She closed down Subway, and we went for a walk in the woods. I asked if she was going to be okay. She said she didn't know, but all this death was making her feel extremely sexual. We sat on a fallen hemlock tree and she pulled a vial out of her pocket. She asked if I'd ever done cocaine before. I said no, but it sounded pretty interesting. We each did a line and my brain felt like it was full of bright pink birds. Then she took off her shorts and we had unprotected sex.

When we finished, she used my shirt to clean herself up and asked if I was hungry. I said sort of, so we went back to Subway, and she made me a BBQ Oven Roasted Chicken Melt. I thanked her for the sandwich and she thanked me for Nash's tooth. I never asked her if she was on birth control and she never asked me how Nash died.

WHAT HAPPENED TO NASH, PART VI

I drove around with Nash for another hour visiting all the places we used to hang out since we'd met on the jungle gym fire engine in the second grade. Plaid Pantry, Taco Bell, the woods by my house, the woods by his house, Aloha High School, Five Oaks Middle School, William Howard Taft Elementary.

At Taft, the bell had just rung and children the size of babies ran toward the building as their teacher blew her whistle and said they weren't going anywhere until they formed a single file line. The children, mostly boys, tried to obey her, but their bodies were full of wonderful energy and they couldn't stop themselves from making obscene gestures.

One boy in particular, a genius, pretended to have an erection the size of a baseball bat, which he massaged for the benefit of anyone willing to watch. The teacher yanked him out of line by his shirt collar and blew her whistle directly into his ear. I watched his joy transform into hatred and knew he'd be in a penitentiary one day trying to figure out where everything went wrong.

I wanted to tell that sadist that she could save the taxpayers of Oregon a lot of money by giving this boy some kind of award for creativity instead of ruining his inner ear, but then I saw the fire engine where I first met Nash, and I started crying.

He was 8 years old and had a crust of snot lining each nostril and a pretty advanced case of pink eye, but when I asked him when he was going to be done hogging the steering wheel of the fire engine, he said, "It's not a fire engine, it's a Naked Lady Finding Machine."

After that we pretty much did everything together until he ate a handful of pills and shot himself like an arrow into the bull's-eye of Jesus.

WHAT HAPPENED TO NASH,
PART VII

I picked up the cardboard box and walked through the gate to the playground and sat on the fire engine with Nash and looked across the highway to the shopping center that used to be a field of swaying yellow grass and a barn with a sunk-in roof that was supposedly full of bats. I thought about how beautiful life was back then driving around in the Naked Lady Finding Machine and how everything changes and how eventually people die.

I didn't understand it. I just didn't get how this box of gray powder was the same person who thought the afterlife was a Björk video, or the teenager who pushed his big red lips against the microphone and sang "Sitting in a Bathtub with Jean-Paul Sartre," or the snot-nosed kid who for reasons totally unclear to me never had the genius blasted out of him no matter how hard the teacher blew her whistle.

I thought about the Hindu worldview—how we're born over and over and over, trying to get it right each time just so that we don't have to be born anymore—and I thought that was the saddest idea in the world. All I wanted was to not die. To be able to live this one stupid life, only with a reverse button because I wanted one more night with Nash drinking wine out of a box, shouting Allen Ginsberg poems at the top of our lungs.

I was thinking something along these lines when a woman approached, the same teacher who'd just made a mischievous and somewhat lewd student permanently deaf.

WHAT HAPPENED TO NASH, PART VIII

The teacher told me that I couldn't be here. She said that visitors had to go to the principal's office and sign in and get a badge. She said this like I'd already molested two of her students and was catching my breath while I worked up the courage to molest a third.

I was about to tell her what I thought about people like her, but then I saw who she actually was—an extremely angry woman in her mid-to-late 40s in a pantsuit from Nordstrom trying to control the chaos she saw everywhere in the world, mostly inside herself. I saw that she'd never be happy and that no one loved her and that no one would ever love her because she'd been broken a long time ago and that whatever was left of her just wanted to break the spirits of children making obscene gestures involving giant imaginary penises. I saw that she spent her nights alone and that her best friends were the cast of *Seinfeld*, and then I felt so bad that I started apologizing and told her that my best friend died and used to go to school here.

She asked what my friend's name was. I said Nash Derbes. She asked if he was by any chance related to Royce Derbes.

I said that was his older brother. She told me that Royce was one of her all-time favorite students and asked what he was up to these days. I said that from what I understood he was a pretty successful drug dealer up in Yakima and that he'd scored the pills that killed his little brother.

The teacher didn't know what to say about that. I didn't know what to say either, but that was okay because it was time for me to go because I was starting to feel extremely paranoid that Mercedes had AIDS.

I carried Nash under my left arm and drove to 7-11 and called Blackbird and said that I'd just had sex with Mercedes McKechnie without a condom and was pretty sure I had AIDS.

He said, "Dude, you don't have AIDS."

I said, "How do you know?"

He said, "If she'd given you AIDS, you'd know it."

"How?" I asked.

"You'd just know it, man," he said.

WHAT HAPPENED TO NASH, PART IX

Blackbird said we should have one last band practice with Nash before spreading his ashes in the Pacific Ocean. I said that sounded about right, so I drove over to Blackbird's apartment in Multnomah Village. I didn't have my guitar so I played Nash's old acoustic, which only had three strings.

We tried to play an instrumental version of "Which Way to Nowhere?" with the microphone set in front of Nash's ashes like he was singing from beyond the grave, but two verses in I realized that Nash's guitar wasn't even close to being in tune, so I just played the low E, which was actually a double-low A-flat and screamed and Blackbird made Indian sounds by howling and clapping his hand over his mouth in a way that I'm pretty sure was racist against a quarter of his ancestors.

Then I pushed the headstock of Nash's guitar through the sheetrock and kicked a hole in Blackbird's bass drum and swore that I'd never play a musical instrument ever again as long as I lived, and to this day, I've kept my word.

WHAT HAPPENED TO NASH, PART X

We decided the ocean was too far away, so we drove downtown and parked in Chinatown and walked onto the Burnside Bridge carrying Nash's ashes. By then it was sunset and the West Hills blazed pink and orange and cars were backed up leaving the city driven by men in ties who I thought were wasting their lives making other people rich but were actually in love with their own children and doing everything they could to provide for them.

Blackbird said he'd like to read a Sioux prayer before I spread Nash's ashes. I asked him how he just so happened to have a piece of notebook paper in his pocket with a Sioux prayer written on it in the nearly illegible script of a five-year-old.

He said, "Things are beginning to happen to me, Nelson, that you wouldn't even begin to believe."

Then he read the prayer. It went:

Oh, Great Spirit—
Whose voice I hear in the wind
And whose breath gives life to all the world, hear me.

I am small and weak.
I need your strength and wisdom.
Let me walk in beauty and make my eyes behold the red and purple sunset.
Make my hands respect the things you have made
And my ears sharp to hear your voice.
Make me wise so that I may understand the things you have taught my people.
Let me learn the lessons you have hidden in every leaf and rock.
I seek strength, not to be superior to my brother,
But to fight my greatest enemy—myself.
Make me always ready to come to you with clean hands and straight eyes,
So when life fades, as the fading sunset,
My spirit will come to you without shame.

I told Blackbird that was truly and completely beautiful, but wasn't he Cherokee?

He said yes, but he couldn't find a Cherokee prayer on any of the greeting cards at the Healing Wellness Gift Store.

We were both silent for a long time. Then I made my speech. I don't remember exactly what I said, but I think it went, "Fuck you. Fuck you a big one, Nash."

Then I dumped the cardboard box over the bridge and his ashes rained down and I threw the box and the plastic bag and they cartwheeled down into the water. Then it was just me and Blackbird staring down into the Willamette River, that body of water that cuts Portland, Oregon in half, and I couldn't help but think that Nash was gone, but he was just the first of us to cross over and that eventually we'd all join him in whatever Dark Eternity he'd traveled to.

HOW LORETTA AND I FOUND OURSELVES LIVING AS HUSBAND AND WIFE, HIGH ON DRUGS

Loretta figured out pretty quick that she loved screw more than she loved Bennie. Also, she had a pregnancy scare with Eric, and Bennie decided that Loretta wasn't the ideal woman to have around when the world ended. So she and I moved back to Portland and found ourselves together again in Dmitri's basement living as lovers. Junkie lovers high on screw every day of our lives, never healthy enough to have sex, but deeply in love still, sort of, if we ever were.

Our days were nightmares and our evenings were like enemas of glass, but inside the pain was the end of pain and inside of that was a deeper "us," better than ourselves.

Loretta and I often talked about how our new junkie bodies were like butterflies in a state of chrysalis. We felt ourselves becoming kinder, more compassionate people, even as our teeth fell out and our arms became pastures of laceration and staphylococcus. Still, we clung to the belief that any second we'd crack through these mortal coils and emerge slimy with colorful wings.

One night Loretta overdosed and I drove her to the

hospital. I lied and said that I was her brother so they wouldn't think I was just some junkie. Then the nurse handed me a wastebasket, and I realized that I couldn't stop vomiting and that I seemed to be overdosing as well.

Another night we got so high I broke into our next-door neighbor's house and stole their television so we could watch *The Simpsons*. I asked Loretta where I should put it. She said on top of the TV, which is how we discovered that we already had a TV.

HOW TO STEAL USED MEDICAL EQUIPMENT

Screw was expensive, so I started stealing medical equipment. It was easy because Sandy, my loading dock supervisor, had been diagnosed with cancer and was dying in a house on Martin Luther King Jr. Boulevard. There was nobody to join me on my cigarette breaks or give me relationship advice or prevent me from becoming an unrepentant crook.

Whenever a truck arrived with an expensive and not-too-bulky shipment, I'd sign for it using my left hand instead of my right. When the driver pulled away, I'd push the dolly out to my car and unload it into my trunk.

That was it.

If my boss noticed the discrepancy, I claimed the drivers of all those delivery vans were heroin addicts who sold medical equipment for drug money. I said they'd learned to forge my signature, but not very well. As proof, I suggested that he compare the signatures on the invoices.

He checked and confirmed they were different.

I said of course they're different and offered to kill the drivers who were stealing from us.

He said, "No way, José. Let me take care of it."

I feigned extreme disappointment that he hadn't given me the green light to murder the men I was framing for the robberies I was committing.

I was pretty certain that the only truth in the world came in the form of a powder I mixed with water, boiled, and injected into the crook of my arm, but if I had been concerned with ethics, I would've reckoned myself some kind of Robin Hood. Not because I stole from the rich (Bossman Tate drove a rusted-out VW Rabbit) or because I gave to the poor (Loretta and I owned two televisions), but because I was fucking over the fucker that fucked over Sandy.

SANDY

While Sandy was having her gallbladder removed, they found cancer in her spleen. When they cut her open to pull out the cancer, they found more cancer. When I heard the news, I imagined her surrounded by all the medical equipment she'd spent her entire life loading and unloading.

The problem was that she wasn't surrounded by any. About a week after her second surgery, Sandy started receiving medical bills with unusual messages printed on them. Things like:

1. There seems to be a problem with your claim.
2. We've been unable to track down the account associated with the policy number provided.
3. This insurance company doesn't exist.

It turned out that our boss was running a scam. A few months earlier, he'd discovered that the credit card debt he'd been shuffling around most of his adult life had finally caught up with him and he was about to lose his house. At the same time, the company's medical insurance plan came up for renewal and he was astonished to find out how much rates were being jacked.

I don't know whether a light bulb actually appeared above his head, but at the weekly team meeting of Tate Medical Supply & Co., he informed his full-time employees that he was switching insurance providers from Kaiser to Ajax Life, a relatively unknown but (he assured them) more than adequate policy provider. He kept his house and everything seemed hunky dory, as long as no one ever got sick or went to the doctor for a checkup.

So instead of having a 50/50 chance at beating her disease, Sandy was a corpse rotting in a La-Z-Boy with her niece Rosie sitting beside her reading Sandy's favorite Bible passages, hoping Jesus might provide what Ajax Life hadn't.

I visited her once and it was awful. Unlike Nash who'd merrily pursued his death, Sandy enjoyed things like waking up and having a body. She couldn't hide her misery in spite of Jesus' reassurances that the Kingdom of God is within and that the afterlife will be halos and angel wings for those that put their faith in Him.

"I don't want to die," said Sandy. "I'm young."

"You're not going to die," I lied. "You look great."

"I look like shit," she said. "But you look worse. What the hell, Nelson? Are you on drugs?"

I told her that I was. Strong ones. I told her about screw—how it makes you feel like a butterfly, but actually rots out your brain and makes you think it's a good idea to pull out your teeth. I said that Loretta had a thing for incisors, but luckily so far I'd just pulled out molars.

"Loretta?" she said. "What did I tell you about that one?"

"I know I know I know," I said. "But I'm a sucker for freckles. I can't help it. I'm like one of those monkeys who sticks his hand in a hole to steal a nut, then gets stuck because his fist is bigger than the hole he just stuck it in."

She said, "You definitely stuck it in the wrong hole, Nelson."

I lit a cigarette and Sandy said, "My God, you precious child, can I have one of those?"

I handed her a Camel and we smoked and Sandy's niece looked at us with eyes full of judgment.

Sandy said, "What? You're afraid I'm going to get cancer?"

Then she said, "Nelson, I have something I need to tell you. I married a man with an extremely small penis. What was I thinking? Thirty years. He was a good man, but *so* small."

I didn't know what to say to that. Rosie made the sign of the cross over her blouse.

"It goes by just like *that*," she said, snapping her fingers. "All old people say that, but they're right." Then, "Do you love this woman? This bitch? What's her name? Loretta?"

"I do."

"Good. Love her. Give her your heart and let her shit on it. You think it's bad, but it's the best feeling in the world. Before my husband, I dated a man named Jack and he had a prick the size of my arm. He made love to me slowly, kissing my titties, my pussy, my asshole—everywhere. He made love to all the women in the neighborhood that way and told each of us we were the only one he really loved. When I found out, I thought he was the devil, but here on my deathbed, am I thinking about Howard? No. I'm thinking about Jack with his cock the size of my arm."

I looked at Sandy's arm and thought of the slave from *Hustler*, then felt extremely racist for thinking about slavery in front of a black woman who was dying of cancer.

Sandy said she was sorry to hear that I was a junkie in love with another junkie because she had hopes of setting me up with Rosie here, who in spite of being a devout Christian, wanted nothing more than to marry a man with a big cross who knew how to use it.

Rosie blushed and looked out the window, and for a second I imagined getting clean and marrying her, going to church every Sunday, having mixed-race babies with crosses around their necks. I saw that it would be a good life and considered it for about as long as I considered joining Dmitri's Capoeira studio, which wasn't very long.

TREASURE

After Blackbird and I dumped Nash's remains over the Burnside Bridge, we stole a bottle of peach schnapps and got drunk in the Park Blocks.

Blackbird said, "I'm worried."

"About what?" I asked.

"Loretta," he said. "She's plucking us off one by one."

We finished the schnapps and smashed the bottle and cut our hands open with the jagged glass and became blood brothers and swore that neither of us would talk to Loretta ever again as long as we lived.

Then Blackbird went to the hospital to get stitches, and I found a payphone and called Loretta to see if she was okay.

"Me?" she said. "I'm great!"

I tried to tell her what we'd done with Nash's ashes, but she refused to listen. She said she wasn't interested in that kind of thing anymore.

"What kind of thing?" I asked.

"Wallowing," she said.

"But he died three days ago," I said.

"The sooner you let go," she said, "the sooner you'll start feeling better."

She said she was leaving tomorrow for an organic farm on Orcas Island where she'd secured a job pulling weeds and spreading cow manure over rutabaga fields. Adam, who'd always had a vague interest in nature and thought overalls made him look like Huckleberry Finn, was coming with her.

I asked Loretta if I could see her one last time before she left. She asked if I was interested in watching her and Adam try out a new sex position called "the waterfall" because that's how she planned on spending the evening. I said that sounded pretty bad, and she said, "Okay then. Bye."

With Loretta gone and Hoyt making his own clothes on a spinning wheel and Nash dead, my life was oddly quiet and lonely with only Blackbird to keep me company. We found a one-bedroom apartment in Hillsboro that only charged $400/month, got ourselves library cards, and spent all our time reading.

Blackbird read books like *Black Elk Speaks* and *Lame Deer, Seeker of Visions*. I read biographies of mystical white people like Henry David Thoreau and Vincent van Gogh. We drank canned beer until 3 a.m., woke up at noon, stumbled out to my Corolla, and drove to Coffee People where we sat in the sun, chain-smoking and reading. Every so often, one of us had to go to work to earn money for coffee, beer, and microwave burritos.

It was here at Coffee People that Blackbird met a 15-year-old named Linda who carried around a lunchbox with a dead crow in it. She never said anything as far as I could tell, which I respected, but it made conversation a real bummer.

So I started keeping to myself, going for long walks in the evening, stealing beer from the grocery store, drinking in Bagley Park, watching the sunset, returning to my living room where I read Vincent van Gogh's letters to his brother Theo, trying to block out the sound of Blackbird and Linda's lovemaking, which is apparently where she got over her fear of making noise.

I read the Van Gogh book over the course of a week. It wasn't at all what I expected. Not the ravings of a lunatic but the oddly sane notes of a seeker of God. A young man trying to find his place, failing with women, with money and the church. Who started drawing destitute people gathering coal in a Belgian village one day and couldn't stop.

One night he felt so awful he cut his ear off and gave it to a prostitute. He said, "Keep this like a treasure," then walked to his yellow house holding the side of his head. The blood was hot on his left arm. It came in gushes every time his heart beat. When he finally made it to his bedroom, the smell of linseed was thick from the paintings of sunflowers still drying on the walls. He closed his eyes and bled into the pillow on his rusty yellow bed.

He wasn't in love with her.

He was in love with color.

With his brother's kindness. And with God.

THE TUGBOAT PILOT

The next morning, Blackbird and Linda were having vigorous sex to the pulsing rhythm of a Nine Inch Nails album. I waited for them to finish, expecting them to stumble out of the bedroom, rinse the sex out of their mouths, and ask me what the plan was. Instead Blackbird started reading Pablo Neruda poetry to her and said they should get pregnant and have a baby named Feather.

I decided to go to Coffee People alone, but the Corolla wouldn't start. Every time I turned the key, blue smoke came out from under the hood and the engine made a sound like a soldier dying on a battlefield.

I walked to the bus stop and took the #52 downtown. It was gray and raining and the city seemed to be infested with homeless people suffering from the delusion that I had money and cigarettes. I walked down Burnside saying, "No no no sorry man, I wish," feeling bad for lying, until I couldn't take it anymore and gave my bus money and rumpled pack of Camels to a woman in a tracksuit who said that Jimmy better stop touching her or she'd cut off his balls.

I followed the sidewalk over the bridge, wondering if

child molesters had any idea what they were doing when they touched little girls. Then I thought of 20-year-old Blackbird reading "Full Moon, Fleshy Apple, Hot Moon" to 15-year-old Linda in our shared bedroom and of 9-year-old Loretta hearing the sounds of her father's drunken footsteps in the middle of the night, and suddenly it seemed like the whole world was perverted and desperate and alone and I hated everyone and thought about jumping off the bridge and joining Nash in whatever Dark Eternity he'd discovered.

But when I looked over the edge, I saw a tugboat piloted by a man with a handlebar mustache.

I decided that if it ever really got that bad, instead of killing myself, I'd become a tugboat captain with ten cats on my boat, each named after a philosopher.

Friedrich.

Søren.

Immanuel.

Jean-Paul.

Jean-Jacques.

Socrates.

Lao-Tzu.

Camus.

Plato.

And Confucius.

I'd spend my life on blue water with seagulls and rope and clouds, watching humanity drift by on either side—fighting and struggling and fucking and dying—while I passed through the middle of it all, smiling inwardly or just killing time until it was over.

WHAT LORETTA LEARNED
ON ORCAS ISLAND

When I got home, Blackbird and Linda were sitting on the floor playing chess. Blackbird said, "Loretta's here!" without looking up from Linda's king's gambit.

I found her at the kitchen table, head in hands, sobbing. Her eyes looked like somebody'd rubbed raspberries all over them.

She almost jumped when she saw me, then said, "Nelson, we need to talk."

We went outside onto the balcony. I waited for her to explain, but we just sat there, silently smoking cigarettes.

Finally Loretta said, "Will you please just make love to me?"

The way she said it, I'd never heard anything so sad in my life, not since Hoyt stuck his dad's gun in my mouth and said, "Bang!"

I told her that I didn't have any condoms.

She said it didn't matter, and a minute later I was inside of her and she was whispering, "I love you I love you I love you."

Instead of whispering, "I love you too," I watched a

stellar jay in the gutter of our apartment building cleaning itself in rainwater, its fierce black eye filled with the darkness of the universe.

I asked Loretta if I should pull out.

She said no and bit me for the duration of my orgasm so hard it drew blood.

I didn't understand what just happened, and there seemed to be mothers and children playing in the park adjacent to our apartment building in full view of the sin we'd just committed, so we quickly returned to our pants.

Loretta took a deep breath and said, "I'm pregnant."

"Jesus," I said. "That was fast!"

"No," she said. "It's Nash's baby."

She said that as soon as she got to Orcas Island, she started puking. She thought it was all that clean air mixed with the smell of manure, but Adam told her that the only time he'd ever seen anyone puke that much was his sister before her abortion. So Loretta took a pregnancy test and it came out positive. She said there was slim to no chance it was Adam's baby because she and Adam used condoms every time, but her and Nash had all kinds of issues because Nash's dick flipped up against his belly button when he got hard, which made sex incredibly difficult, and the only way they could make it work was with a lot of lube and no rubbers.

Then she confessed that since the baby's conception, she'd done magic mushrooms thirteen times and was afraid she'd microwaved her baby's brain.

"Your baby's fine," I said.

"How do you know?" she asked.

"Think of all those babies born in the 1960s."

She smiled and grabbed me and said she was sick of all this shit and just wanted to be normal and raise her baby to be an accountant.

"What about Adam?" I asked.

"He joined the farmer's jug band," she said. "They just got signed by Virgin Records. They're amazing."

A week later we moved into her Grams's trailer and started drinking a lot of carrot juice, brainstorming baby names, and reading *What to Expect When You're Expecting*.

JESUS LOVES YOU

After Sandy died, I stole pretty much every shipment that came into Tate Medical Supply & Co., hoping that the red number on the company's balance sheet would more or less resemble a middle finger.

One afternoon the Corolla was weighed down with so much stolen property that I couldn't get it above 45 mph. I pulled off the freeway at the Broadway exit, and at the red light, noticed a homeless man holding a sign that said:

DOING WELL
EVERYTHING FINE

I'd seen signs like, "Even a smile helps" or "Go ahead, pelt a bum with a quarter," but I'd never seen a homeless man advertising his contentment.

I dug around the cup holder, found 75 cents, rolled down the window, and said, "Hey bub. Here's 75 cents. Take it."

He shook his head and said no thanks. As he said it, I noticed that his beard was clean and that his torn shirt was actually a polo with a Ralph Lauren jockey on the breast.

He had a cashmere sweater tied around his waist and was absentmindedly fingering the strings of a Dunlop tennis racket.

"Seriously man," he said. "Keep the money. You look like you need it."

Then he reached into the bushes, produced a black leather briefcase, opened it, and handed me a foot-tall porcelain statue of the Virgin Mary.

"Take this," he said. "Jesus loves you."

"Isn't this the Virgin Mary?" I asked.

"They were out of Jesus," he said.

The light turned green, and I pulled away deeply confused and a little creeped out and decided to tell Loretta all about it and ask if it was some sort of sign, but when I got home, she was prostrate on the living room floor in a puddle of blood, her skin blue as Krishna, the eighth incarnation of Vishnu.

TINY TOON ADVENTURES

She'd overdosed again and hit her head on a Cooper Surgical CS1600 Digital Colposcopy System. I looked down at her and couldn't believe it. She was dead. It was like the first time she cheated on me with Nash all over again. He finally had her in his ashy embrace, that ratdick bastard. But just in case she wasn't dead, I put my mouth on her mouth and breathed into her lungs and hit her on the tit with my fist.

Nothing happened.

I looked around to see if there was anything I could use to save her life and realized that our apartment was full of stolen medical equipment. I plugged in the colposcopy machine and tried to examine her cervix, then realized I wasn't thinking straight and snorted a line of screw. Then I was in the Other Country thinking about skulls and butterflies.

Luckily, I started to pass out and hit my head on a Philips Heart Start FRx Defibrillator, which reminded me that Loretta's heart had stopped and here was a way to start it.

I turned it on and heard the electric whir of the paddles charging and yelled, "Clear!" like in the movies and placed the paddles between her tits, and then her chest bucked up in the air like it did when she had a penetration-only orgasm.

I checked to see if she was breathing, but she was dead, so I did another line of screw and Immanuel Kant appeared and told me to pray to Jesus and ask Him to save Loretta.

I thought Immanuel Kant was crazy, but then I realized that I was high on drugs and he wasn't.

So I went out to my car and got the statue of the Virgin Mary and said, "Jesus—I mean Mary—please save my girlfriend." I begged her and fell on the ground and sobbed and said that if she saved Loretta, I'd never do screw again and I'd become a tugboat captain and dedicate my life to helping homeless people, giving them polo shirts and tennis rackets, whatever they needed to not suffer so much.

When I finished my prayer, I went inside and Loretta was sitting on the couch watching *Tiny Toon Adventures*.

When she saw me, she asked how work was today.

"Good," I said.

THE GENIE

I showed Loretta the statue of the Virgin Mary.

She said, "How much do you think it's worth?"

I said, "I'm pretty sure it's some kind of wish-granting genie, so probably a lot."

She didn't understand, so I rubbed the statue and asked it for a million dollars.

Nothing happened.

Loretta asked if I'd done screw today.

I said, "Yes, twice, when you were dead."

She said, "Jesus, it must've been the good stuff."

I said, "I have no idea what's good or bad, but I think I made a pact with the universe and now it's my moral duty to become a tugboat captain."

Loretta got frustrated and said that a statue of the Virgin Mary was a lot harder to sell than an Edan M3B Capnograph Monitor.

I said I thought she was missing the point and should be grateful that I'd saved her life.

She said she wished I'd saved her a little bit of whatever I'd snorted.

I got mad at Loretta and wished I'd let her die.

HOW TO BUY SCREW IN PORTLAND, OREGON

Loretta said she wouldn't testify against me in court when my boss figured out that I was the one stealing all of his medical equipment if I scored us some really strong screw. I was starting to worry about that, so I said okay.

I couldn't get a hold of Rico, our usual drug dealer, so I called Hoyt, who'd recently forgiven me for everything that happened back in '96 because he'd started mainlining screw, which makes you think you're a butterfly capable of saving the world.

I asked if he knew where I could score some screw.

He said, "Yeah, but only the strong stuff."

I said, "That's what Loretta and I like, the strong stuff."

He said, "Oh God Loretta, what a marvel of a woman."

I said, "About those drugs."

He said, "I mean the super strong stuff. The black stuff."

I said, "There's black screw?"

He said, "My God, have you ever become a baby and crawled backwards into your mother's vagina?"

I said, "Sort of."

He said, "There's no *sort of* about the black stuff."

So I drove over to Hoyt's and discovered that he'd

recovered from his hunger strike by becoming fantastically obese. He didn't have a single tooth in his head and his arms were wrapped up like mummies.

I said, "Jesus, Hoyt, you got fat. What happened to your arms?"

"Side effect," he said.

I nodded, but didn't really register what he'd said until five hours later when Loretta was writhing on the floor trying to cut her arms open with an EXACTO knife.

SAVING THE WORLD

I tied Loretta to a chair using two extension cords and the belt of a terrycloth bathrobe. I was extremely high and 100% convinced that Loretta was trying to kill herself because I hadn't fulfilled my promise to become a tugboat captain and save the world. I wasn't sure how to become a tugboat captain, but the city was full of homeless people who didn't seem to be doing very well, so I gave Loretta a kiss, said, "Please don't slice your arms open," and loaded the Virgin Mary statue into the passenger seat of my car.

It was pouring rain and the rain on the windshield made the road look like drippy black monsters, but Jesus was full of strange and cunning magic and made two beams of light shoot out the front of my car.

I parked in Chinatown and walked around, telling people they were saved. Nobody believed me. They were suffering from mental illnesses too profound and deeply rooted in childhood to be cured by a junkie waving around a Virgin Mary statue.

I told them that they all had houses now and that their suffering was a thing of the past. A naked man sitting in a pile of his own shit looked up and said, "Right on, brother!"

I told them that I'd appreciate it if they all got better now because I was scared my girlfriend was going to die.

They said things like, "Be quiet, man, we're trying to sleep."

Then the drugs wore off and I saw that the homeless people were still homeless and that none of them were wearing polos or holding tennis rackets. I walked among them and understood that the world was full of Lorettas and that to be a Loretta was to suffer and that not everyone was lucky enough to know a way out other than shooting drugs that tricked their brains into releasing chemicals associated with childhoods happier than their own.

A woman, probably in her 40s, slept on a piece of cardboard clutching a naked Barbie. A Native American in a San Francisco 49ers sleeping bag had a nose like it'd been broken a thousand times, but his braided black hair was softer than a girl's. I tucked a dollar bill into the jacket of a Vietnam vet with a safety clip where his knee should have been; the way his silver beard cascaded from his VFW hat reminded me of Columbia Gorge waterfalls.

I wasn't saving the world, but I thought maybe there was some way I could help these people. But I was scared of them. The sores on their hands. The crumbs on their mouths. They disgusted me. I had some Christlike idea I was going to help them, but really I was reveling in the thoroughness of their destruction.

I thought of Vincent van Gogh. Short, serious, one-eared. Holding his belly because he'd just shot himself, the sky above him a mess of crows.

Where does it go? That feeling you had. The feeling we want reading stories of your suffering. You, the people Christ talked about when he wasn't talking about us.

THE SONOSITE

At work Monday, Tate found me on the loading dock and said he had a problem. A few weeks ago he'd ordered a brand new Sonosite 180 Plus Ultrasound. Ordinarily he didn't like dealing in new equipment, but he was doing a favor for a long-time customer, Dr. Tobias Corn. The problem was Corn never received his Sonosite. Tate went through his invoices and it appeared that I was the one who'd received the shipment and the signature seemed legit.

I realized my slip-up and accused the delivery people of improving their forgery skills.

Tate said, "Yeah, the thing is I'm good friends with Ed Brunhoff who sells these customized ultrasounds, and he delivered the unit himself. I called him up yesterday and asked who received it and he said a kid named Nelson. I sent him a photo of you from the company picnic and he said you were the one."

I said, "That's mighty big talk coming from a guy running a health insurance Ponzi scheme."

Tate said, "This very well may be a case of the pot calling the kettle black, but I have enough money to hire an attorney, whereas I'm pretty sure you're a junkie without a dime."

I asked if he'd ever eaten a brown asshole and if not would he like to?

He said he just wanted the Sonosite back and all the other medical equipment I stole or he was going to call the police.

$970 WORTH OF SCREW

I drove straight home without clocking out and told Loretta the gig was up.

"What gig?" she whistled through the gaps that used to be her teeth.

"This gig," I said, waving my arm around the living room. "The medical supplies. Tate knows everything."

She helped me load the stolen goods into the Corolla and we drove to MedPDX, Tate Medical Supply & Co.'s chief rival in Portland, Oregon. I told Hal, my buyer, that I was having a red light special—he could have everything in my car minus Loretta for $1000.

He asked how much if Loretta was included.

I said she wasn't for sale.

Loretta said, "How much would you be willing to pay?"

Hal said, "Honey, what happened to your teeth?"

We spent $970 on 97 dime bags of black screw and the other $30 on two 2x4s, a hammer, and ten nails. Then we drove back to Dmitiri's house, barricaded ourselves in the basement, lined up the dime bags on the table, gave each other a kiss, and got ready to ingest way too much of the strongest drug in the world.

GIVING BIRTH TO A DEAD MAN'S BABY

Loretta said she wanted me in the room with her when she gave birth to her baby girl. I said I was pretty certain I'd pass out and vomit all over the floor. She said pretty please, and seven months later I stood in the corner of a delivery room at St. Vincent's Hospital watching a doctor wave a needle around, trying to jam it into Loretta's spine when she wasn't looking.

Loretta spoke in tongues, assuring him that she wasn't a drug addict and that if he put that needle in her, she'd most assuredly rip off his testicles. Then she moaned and opened her legs and a black sun began to rise inside of what was increasingly becoming something totally different than a vagina.

The nurses said, "You're doing a great job, sweetie!"

I said, "Thanks! I was worried I was going to pass out, but I feel pretty good, actually."

The doctor looked at his gold watch and said, "Things aren't moving along fast enough. I want to cut this baby out of you."

Loretta had a contraction, somewhere in the middle of which she promised to stick a knife in the doctor's left eye if he even hinted at that possibility one more time.

At some point I lost my mind and started praying for everyone in the entire world, and once I started I couldn't stop.

I've read four books by Friedrich Nietzsche, two by Søren Kierkegaard, 50 pages of *Critique of Pure Reason*, most of Plato, and all of *Zen and the Art of Motorcycle Maintenance* by Robert Pirsig, but when I saw the look on Loretta's face as that tiny human being popped out of her, I knew that not a single word in any of those books meant anything. That whatever life is, it's bigger than words, and all we can do is live it, just like our parents lived it and their parents and their parents.

The doctors needed to do some tests on Loretta and the nurses thought I was the father, so they handed Allie to me.

I was 20 years old and holding a newborn baby was so much different than being stoned that I started crying. Loretta saw me crying, and even though a doctor had his hand inside her vagina, testing the integrity of her vaginal wall, she started crying too. We were both crying and I was praying and I'm still praying for that poor child, wherever she is, and I hope I was right when I said all those drugs Loretta took didn't microwave your tiny brain.

THE BUTTERFLY HUNTERS, PART I

We dumped 97 bags of screw into a heaping pile that looked eerily like what Nash looked like right before I dumped him in the Willamette River. Then we cut the mound into lines and snorted them one by one into our brains through a rolled up $20 bill. I thought about all the bills I'd thrown in Loretta's face when I got my first paycheck from Tate Medical Supply & Co., saying, "Do you love me now? Do you love me? How much money until you love me?"

Then Immanuel Kant rode up on a Huffy and asked me what I was doing.

I said, "I seem to be ingesting way too much of the strongest drug in the world."

He said, "Right on man, right on."

I hopped onto the back of his bike, wrapped my arms around his waist, and we rode through a valley of inky darkness.

Immanuel said this one time he wrote a book called the *Critique of Pure Reason* while he was in the valley of NO WORDS and it was totally crazy.

I told him I tried to read it one time and it felt like trying to masturbate with a hand grenade.

He took that as a compliment, and then my junkie skin cracked open, and I emerged slimy with colorful wings.

I said, "It's about time I got rid of that disgusting skin. I was starting to think it was a bad idea taking all these drugs."

Immanuel said, "The only problem is now you're a butterfly and you have to watch out for the Butterfly Hunters."

I asked him what he was talking about, but he was gone and I was sitting on the floor of my living room in a puddle of urine, and my hands and face seemed to be covered in powder.

"Loretta!" I yelled. "Are you still alive?"

She said that she was, but she couldn't find any razor blades.

I said, "Immanuel Kant told me the Butterfly Hunters are coming!"

"Fuck those ratdick Butterfly Hunters!" she said. "I'm gonna cut my arms and legs open with a razor blade and show them who's boss. Oh! Here it is."

I was glad Loretta had a plan for dealing with those ratdicks, but I felt responsible since I was the one who'd turned into a butterfly. I went to the door and listened and seemed to hear Dmitri speaking English, telling someone who sounded like a Butterfly Hunter that the junkies lived in the basement.

I couldn't believe it! He was a traitor. And to think I'd almost joined his Capoeira studio.

Luckily we'd already barricaded the door, but I thought I'd just as well stay there and turn their hatred into love with the benevolent power of my wings.

Loretta said, "Honey bun, I think I'm dying."

I said, "What makes you say that?"

"Look," she said.

I went into the bathroom and found her in the bathtub, totally naked. She'd cut her arms and legs wide open with a razor blade and seemed to be yanking her veins out and piling them on the bathmat.

"I can't get them all," she said. "I feel weak."

"Keep cutting," I said. "You'll get them."

ALLIE, PART I

Loretta was in the hospital for two days after the baby was born. Then one morning, the doctor said, "Alright, you two. Looks like it's time to go home."

"Wait," said Loretta. "What's going to happen to my baby?"

"She's going with you," said the doctor.

"Oh."

When we got back to the trailer, Grams looked up from the couch. She had a mud mask on and cucumber slices over her eyes.

"This is my baby," said Loretta.

"I've got a mask on, dear."

"Don't you want to meet your great-granddaughter?"

"It's a baby," said Grams. "She'll still be here when *The Price is Right* is over."

We laid Allie on Loretta's bed. Wrapped in her swaddling clothes, she looked exactly like a burrito.

"What do we do now?" asked Loretta.

"What do you mean?" I asked.

"I mean, should we play with it?"

"She's sleeping."

"When she wakes up, I mean."

"I think you just feed her," I said.

"Again?" said Loretta. "I fed her this morning."

"Yeah, I think that's just something you do now."

Loretta didn't know how to take care of a baby and didn't want to learn. A few days later we were sitting in the kitchen, me reading *What to Expect the First Year* while Loretta tried to feed Allie a spoonful of honey because her tits hurt and she was trying to wean her baby at the ripe age of six days.

I read a paragraph that said you weren't supposed to feed babies honey, but Loretta didn't believe me. I showed her the bright red "Danger Alert! Botulism" header on page 187.

She said that in the olden days kids survived just by sucking the nutrients out of strips of leather cut from a horse's saddle.

THE BUTTERFLY HUNTERS, PART II

I heard a crash followed by what sounded like a human being complaining that a couple screwheads seemed to have barricaded the door. Luckily I knew the truth—we were under siege by an unimaginative Butterfly Hunter intent on smashing our Virgin Mary statue because he was in favor of homelessness.

Loretta said something from the bathroom, but I couldn't understand what because her mouth was full of blood. She sounded like a pot of soup bubbling on the stove.

I went to the bathroom and said, "What's that, honey bun?"

She just looked at me like, *My God, Nelson, what the hell have I done?*

She was pale and her eyes kept rolling into the back of her head.

I remembered Billy's calm in a situation almost exactly like this one, so I pulled down on Loretta's lower eyelids and quoted him, saying, "Stay with me, Loretta. You look funny."

She couldn't speak English because she was dying, but I had a pretty profound realization at that moment that the only way the Butterfly Hunters could take us was in our bodies and that Loretta seemed to be leaving hers.

They had two choices: take her skin or her veins. Neither of them was Loretta.

ALLIE, PART II

In retrospect I realize that Loretta was suffering from postpartum depression just like her mother when she poured boiling soup over her newborn's wailing body. Loretta didn't pour soup over Allie, but sometimes in the morning after Allie'd been up all night screaming, she'd say things like, "Remember that lady who drove a car off a cliff with her kids in the back seat? I bet for those few seconds before the car hit the ground, she felt like she was flying."

I didn't think about it much until I came home from work one day and found Allie in a car seat on the kitchen table with a note safety-pinned to her that said, "Out for a bit. Feed her?" There was a bear-shaped container of honey on the table and a spoon.

Grams had left her own note safety-pinned to Allie that said, "Came home and found baby here but I have bingo tonight. You got this, Nelson?"

I drove to Target with Allie in the back seat and bought some baby formula, then drove home and warmed it on the stove. By then Allie was screaming so violently her tiny face muscles looked like they were about to rip apart. When the milk was ready, I fed it to her and she drank it so desperately she choked and it shot out of her nose. I told her to slow down and take a chill pill. I said that I was doing the very best I could and that I was fully aware that my very best was still kind of shitty.

I tried to think of a story to tell her, but the only one I could think of involved a mother driving her car off a cliff with her children in the back seat, and then I thought about *Thelma & Louise*, how the movie ends right as they drive their Ford Thunderbird into a canyon, and I prayed the children in the back seat of that mother's car didn't feel anything, that their movie ended early too.

The whole time I was thinking these thoughts, I was bouncing Allie, and it occurred to me that it was quiet and I looked down and saw that she was asleep and that she was the most perfect, beautiful thing in the whole world.

THE BUTTERFLY HUNTERS,
PART III

Loretta stopped doing normal things like speak, move, and breathe, and it occurred to me that she was dead. I was dead too, but the Butterfly Hunters would probably think I was alive because I still had a body. I wondered if I should yank my veins out and pile them on the bathmat to show those ratdicks who was boss, but as I was weighing the pros and cons of this decision, the basement door exploded and a giant metal penis stuck through. Jesus Christ, I should have known! The Butterfly Hunter was a 20' cast-iron slave seeking revenge for all the shitty things that happened in Brazil two hundred years ago.

I didn't want to be anywhere near that morally-justified monster when he wreaked vengeance on the sugar plantation owners of the world, some of which were my ancestors, so I locked myself in the bathroom with Loretta and told her that I was sorry for all the bad things I'd done to her, like telling her I was a virgin when really I'd had sex with two women, and ruining her Montana vacation by sending her a suicide note, and repeatedly pestering her with ridiculous questions like, *Am I or am I not loveable?*

But mostly for thinking it was a good idea locking ourselves in this basement with $970 worth of drugs.

Just as I was finishing my apology, I noticed a dime bag we'd missed on the soap dish, and it occurred to me that if I snorted it, there was a pretty good chance all my problems would go away.

So I snorted it and got so high I became a skyscraper and a flock of seagulls flew by with the sunset on their wings, and I thought, *My God this piece of shit world sure is pretty sometimes.*

Then my mom showed up and pulled down her underwear and said, "Hide in here, Nelson."

I said, "No way, Mom. I'm tired of hiding from my problems."

She said, "Do you realize there's a Butterfly Hunter outside and a dead girlfriend in the bathtub?"

I said, "Mom, I'm not a kid anymore. I'm a man now."

Then I realized that was the whole problem right there, and I started cutting off my penis.

ALLIE, PART III

Loretta apologized for leaving me alone with Allie. She said she joined a mothering group that met every night of the week from 5 p.m. until midnight and you weren't supposed to bring your baby.

I said that sounded like a negligence group.

She said, "Nelson, can you just try to support me for once?"

And so the following evening and every evening after, she armed me with a bottle of milk that she'd pumped out of her breasts and a $5 bill for "expenses."

I thought about it and realized that we hadn't had sex since that time on the balcony and that I wasn't Loretta's boyfriend, but her extremely cheap nanny. But I couldn't stand the thought of Allie screaming bloody murder in her Johnny Jump-Up while Grams watched TV, since Grams made it clear that she'd been down this road twice already and if she had to go down it a third, she made zero promises the baby wouldn't end up in adult films one day.

I took Allie to the park and pushed her on the baby swing and traded strategies with other mothers for dealing with diaper rash and the discomforts of teething, but no matter what I did, she cried all the time because her mom was at a mothering group trying to learn how to become a better mother. I bounced her up and down, whispering, "I love you. I love you so freaking much," but she choked on her own spit and vomited, and the only thing that seemed to calm her down was taking her for walks.

It was late spring and the flowers were blooming red and yellow and blue in people's gardens. We walked around the trailer park looking in people's windows, watching them watch television. If somebody noticed us, I lifted Allie's tiny hand and waved at them, which made them smile and made us seem less like peeping Toms and more like heroes trying to spread joy in a miserable world.

As I marched Allie around, I told her everything I knew about life, which wasn't much. I said that as far as I could tell, people were always making bad decisions that made their lives worse, and the main reason they made these bad choices was love. I said that everybody I knew was constantly falling in love with the wrong person and usually that person was her mother. I told her that the only way to live was to jump in and feel everything, even though that meant being annihilated.

She didn't understand a word I said, but it didn't matter because taking care of Allie was one of those choices that proved my point.

There was an explosion of thunder in the purple distance, and I heard the sound of a man and woman making love through the open window of a trailer and thought, *Here we go again.*

THE BUTTERFLY HUNTERS, PART IV

When they barged into the bathroom and found us, the joke was on them. They were just men with radios calling for backup. We were simian angels making love to our own darkness.

ALLIE, PART IV

It turned out there was no such thing as a five-to-midnight mothering group. Loretta was sneaking off with her new boyfriend Ken, who she'd met when he accidentally walked into a changing room at the Cherry Sprout Mama Boutique on Hawthorne Boulevard where she was getting measured for a custom breast suction pump that would accommodate her scar tissue.

Ken's 8-months pregnant wife was trying on a Babybjörn in the adjacent room, but when he saw by mistake where Loretta's freckles ended and her scar tissue began, something died in him in a place so deep he asked Loretta what she was doing.

"Having my breasts measured," she said.

"I mean after that," he whispered.

"What did you have in mind?"

They ditched the wife and drove to Council Crest, where they made vigorous love in the back seat of his Taurus listening to The Doors' "Riders on the Storm."

When they were done, they smoked hashish and Ken told her his lifelong dream of doing peyote in the desert with a shaman. Loretta said the thing about dreams is they don't go chasing themselves.

They never made it to the desert, but a couple months later, Loretta scored some peyote buttons, which they ate before going to the Family Fun Center to play Laser Tag. Loretta refused to wear a helmet and got shot in the eye with a laser beam and had a religious experience wherein she realized that the only thing that mattered in life was raising her daughter to be a good person.

She talked Ken into driving her home, even though everywhere he looked, he saw neon buffalo.

It was 2 p.m. when they arrived at Grams's trailer. I was at the record store working a short shift, entrusting Grams to take care of Allie for a few hours. But when Loretta walked in the front door, she found her daughter in a car seat on the kitchen table with a note safety-pinned to her onesie that said, "Sorry Nelson, forgot how much I hate the sound of screaming babies. Went to a movie."

Loretta grabbed Allie.

Ken said, "Where next, honey bun?"

She said, "To make your dreams come true."

They drove east over Mt. Hood headed for the high desert, but somewhere near Rhododendron, the peyote wore off, and Loretta said she was super jonesing for a double bacon cheeseburger. They stopped at Dairy Queen and forgot Allie in the car. It was 92 degrees and she would have died if a woman hadn't noticed her cooking in the back seat and called 911.

WHAT THEY ACTUALLY FOUND

The Butterfly Hunters were actually the police who'd been tipped off that our apartment was full of stolen medical equipment. They didn't find any, but they did find a lot of empty Ziploc bags and a shrine in the living room surrounding a statue of the Virgin Mary. She had a piece of notebook paper scotch-taped to her face with words written on it in #2 pencil:

SAVE US MAMA JESUS
WE DON'T KNOW
WHAT WE'RE DOING

Loretta was in the bathtub floating in sixty percent of her blood. She wasn't dead, but she had lacerations up and down her arms and was in an advanced state of shock.

I was naked on the toilet trying to cut off my own penis with the wrong side of a razor blade.

ALLIE, PART V

Loretta didn't tell me about Ken or her peyote visions—
only that Allie was in state custody and we weren't getting
her back. I suggested we hire an attorney. She said, "Nelson,
will you just hold me?"

So I held Loretta while she sobbed with strings of saliva
stretched between her teeth, saying this was a fucked up
world where you couldn't leave your baby in a car for 30
minutes without being deemed an unfit mother. Then she
said she just wanted to get drunk and watch TV and forget
everything, in particular that she'd ever been born.

I drove to 7-11 and bought a six-pack of beer and two
bottles of Boones Ferry and drove home and turned on the
TV.

The Academy Awards were on. Billy Crystal was
telling jokes and famous people in beautiful clothes were
pretending to laugh.

Loretta said all she ever really wanted was to be famous
and have everybody stare at her all the time and say how
perfect she was.

I said, "I think you're perfect."

She said, "Yeah but that doesn't count because you love

me more than you should."

Then the lights in the Shrine Auditorium dimmed, and an awkward man in a white suit walked onto the stage holding an acoustic guitar. He sang so quietly we had to turn up the volume, and right away it was clear that Elliott Smith didn't belong at the Oscars or anywhere on TV or anywhere on earth. He was here by accident like a monarch butterfly flying through a beer commercial.

Loretta held her breath and squeezed my wrist.

I said, "I think that's the guy from Heatmiser."

Loretta started crying and said she wanted things to be different from now on, and two weeks later we moved in with her cousin.

THE GOOD SAMARITAN

We spent a week in St. Vincent's ICU, then moved down two floors and over a building to the psychiatric ward. I wasn't totally clear whether or not we were free to leave, but Sergeant Pierce informed me that I'd been charged with grand larceny and would stand trial as soon as I was deemed physically and mentally sound enough to understand the instructions of a judge. He read me my Miranda rights while I sat in a wheelchair staring out the window, watching an orange-crowned warbler make a nest in the upper branches of a Douglas fir.

The doctors assured me that I wasn't allowed to see Loretta under any circumstances. Due to the nature of her injuries, she was on suicide watch and visits were strictly limited to family.

I said, "Have you ever met her family?"

A few days later I saw a man in a blue uniform talking to one of my doctors in the hallway and knew they were about to let me out, because as much as I tried to complain that my brain felt like a rowboat floating on a vast ocean of liquid shit, they kept catching me watching *Will & Grace* reruns, which they assured me was an unmistakable sign of mental health.

When the doctor and police officer disappeared, I tiptoed into the hallway with my blue hospital gown cinched around my waist and peeped into various windows until I found a freckled girl in leather restraints in a room with all the sharp edges conspicuously removed.

Loretta was heavily sedated but as beautiful as ever, perhaps more beautiful because she was pale from screw withdrawal, which made her freckles look like Fruit Loops floating in milk.

I squeezed her hand.

She opened her eyes.

I said, "My God, Loretta. What the hell have we done?"

She smiled and tried to talk, but her mouth was too dry. I found a paper cup dispenser and filled a cup full of water and poured it slowly into Loretta's mouth. She coughed and I wiped her mouth with a tissue since her wrists were fastened to the metal rails that ran along the side of the hospital bed.

"I'm in love," she said.

Her eyes seemed to be swimming in and out of consciousness, but the smile on her lips was unmistakable.

"With who?" I asked.

"Dr. Englund. He's been helping me to understand that my addiction and self-destruction are a stress disorder dating back to my unhealthy home environment as a child."

"I could have told you that," I said.

"He has a house in the Cayman Islands. We're going to get away from all this shit, Nelson. Get well for the first time. I mean *really* well. Not just like swapping one drug for another, but you know—healthy. Facing my shit. Really facing it. He says I'm courageous. He says I'm like a warrior with a body covered in orange stars."

"Have you slept with him?" I asked.

"Please don't tell anyone, Nelson. He could get in serious trouble."

I saw the plastic IV tube running from the saline drip into Loretta's arm and thought about wrapping it around her neck and showing her what grace looks like when you finally quit lying. Instead I gave her a kiss on the lips and said, "Wear sunscreen down there."

She smiled a window of missing teeth and I left her and that was the end of me and Loretta.

THE 312 TIMES WE HAD SEX

We had a lot of sex in 1996. Like, twice-a-day sex. That lasted from June through November, when we started having our issues. June, July, August, September, October. Five months. Let's say thirty days each, times two, times five. That's 300 times. That seems like a lot of sex, but when I add up everything else, I can't get past 312, which means that by November of 1996 I'd already had 96% of the sex I'd ever have with Loretta. If I had a time machine and went back and warned 19-year-old Nelson of this rather sad fact, I'm sure 19-year-old Nelson would tell 37-year-old Nelson to go fuck himself, then secretly worry that one of them— either him or Loretta—was about to die.

But neither of us died. Everything else happened. Mostly Nash committing suicide and then screw.

But it isn't about quantity. I love my wife. I truly, deeply love her, but I can't help it if sometimes—when she's gone for the weekend at her sister's in Seattle or out late with her girlfriends—I lie on the bed with the windows open feeling the warm summer air blow over my naked body, remembering.

Like the time I went over to Loretta's after work and

KEVIN MALONEY

found her sitting on the roof of the trailer smoking a Swisher Sweet, drinking a 22oz hazelnut-flavored beer with her Grams's cat Lincoln on her lap. I climbed up the ladder and sat next to her, looking out into the distance. The aspen leaves were twirling green coins and the clouds were gray and pink and the sun made a gold candy wrapper on the horizon.

"Cigar, huh?" I asked.

She didn't answer. The only sound was Lincoln purring, and in the distance a train.

"Do you think we'll ever really go?" she asked.

"Where?"

"Somewhere else."

I snatched the beer out of her hand and took a long sip. "We can do whatever you want, baby."

"But I mean really."

I thought about it and said, "I'm not sure there is an *else*. I'm pretty sure this is all there is."

She looked at me, and I couldn't tell if it was love or the profoundest disappointment in her eyes.

Lincoln stuck his paw out and clawed at nothing.

"I don't think I love you the way you love me," she said.

I nodded.

"I don't think I'll ever love anybody that way."

She put out her cigar, and we went inside and lay on the bed in our underwear, staring at each other. I kept looking for a clue in her hazel eyes, in the place where the brown fibers met the blue fibers, those nebula-like ridges you see when you put your eye up against your girlfriend's eye.

"I want to leave here, Nelson," she said.

"And go where?"

I thought it was a simple question, but I seemed to be tugging on a string that ran all the way from her imagination to the bottom of her soul.

She grabbed me and we made love and maybe it was incredible, but all I remember is darkness followed by the wetness of our lips. I opened my eyes and saw Loretta crying and kissing me with a desperation incongruous with how much she didn't love me.

"What is it, baby?" I asked.

She didn't say, and I'm still trying to figure it out.

BLACKBIRD, PART II

A couple weeks ago I got a call from Blackbird, the last of us to try to date Loretta, the second to get her pregnant, the first to chaperone her to an abortion clinic. I met him outside a coffee shop on Belmont. His hands were red and he kept grabbing the side of his jeans, shaking them, and I knew he was about to say, "Did we do the right thing?" Which brought me back to Loretta a little, her freckles like somebody shot her in the neck with an orange paintball.

We walked to Colonel Summers Park and sat on the bleachers. I knew he loved her or he wouldn't have called me. In me, he was trying to see what life looked like without her, proof that there's an after. Unmaniac eyes, distance, the spirited confidence of my broken spirit. I tried to look happy.

The sky was a mess of fall birds. Two healthy ladies in tapestry skirts pushed a wheelbarrow of rakes into the community garden.

"Where you going first?" I asked.

"Oklahoma. Cherokee pride," he said, running a car key through the rivets in the bleacher seats.

"Know anyone there?" I asked.

He shrugged like it was a ridiculous question.

"The whole time we dated," he said, "she had that braid, only yesterday she didn't."

"You don't want her," I said.

He thought about this and told me, "It's not that simple," which is how men say, "Look at my broken heart. Look at my broken heart, brother, and tell me I don't want her."

Later, we were in a basement sushi joint. The Japanese chef wore a hat made of blue paper. I loved his hands, watching him from the bar where we drank our sake—the way he moved his knife, separating lips of white marble, curling salmon into pink paper.

With a redhead it's the pink parts you look for. The rest is fire at the crown of Jesus' mad heart.

"Thank you," said Blackbird. "Thank you thank you thank you."

Because he was drunk and we were closer to something.

I made him try my unagi and he chewed it with his eyes closed. Then the sushi chef unwrapped an octopus tentacle, and I noticed the gold glint of his wedding band, the lengths he made making mathematics of the ocean. I wanted to give him some part of me and watch him order it, cut me and lay me like wet petals on fists of vinegar rice.

What is it about being 37 that makes less sense as we move closer to the burning core of our women?

Blackbird put his head on my shoulder, his nose in my collar, and took a deep breath.

It occurred to me that this had nothing to do with me and Loretta dating fifteen years ago, but with Karen, my wife, the smell we make in the other world. The world Blackbird almost touched. The smell of our bedroom as I hold Karen's wide hips, and she says, "Are my stretch marks ugly?" and I say, "No, I made them."

"Do you think they'll understand me?" asked Blackbird.

"Who?"

"The Cherokee. I'm only one quarter."

I held up my finger and asked for two ikura, pointed at Blackbird, at his hands that wouldn't stop rapping the table.

The chef nodded. He stopped what he was doing, formed two thumb-sized patties of rice, wrapped them in seaweed, and dropped in the roe.

He set them in front of us.

Blackbird didn't know what to do.

I didn't either, so I ate the whole thing. It tasted like my dad's fingers.

FINGERS

We stood next to the Wilson River. My dad said *here* and cut the old lure from my line and began tying on a new one. The hook stuck in his thumb. He started bleeding but didn't notice. It took him six tries to thread the line through the eye of the hook.

I just want those hands now.

Clean yellow shit from the folds of your baby daughter's vagina, Blackbird, and tell me anything else matters.

ACKNOWLEDGMENTS

Special thanks to Cameron Pierce for shaping this book and guiding it to publication, to Derrick Martin-Campbell, Thad Kenner, Jamey Strathman, and Kirsten Alene Pierce for your invaluable feedback, to Matthew Revert for the badass cover design, to Aaron Burch for your ongoing support, and to Tanna TenHoopen-Dolinsky and Sabine Maloney—my partners in writing and life.

Early versions of material included in *Cult of Loretta* appeared as "Nelson Gets It All" in *Lazy Fascist Review* and "Cult of Loretta" online at *Monkeybicycle*.

ABOUT THE AUTHOR

At times a TJ Maxx associate, grocery store clerk, outdoor school instructor, organic farmer, apprentice electrician, student teacher, and teddy bear salesman, Kevin Maloney currently works as a web developer and writer. He graduated from Johnson State College in Vermont. His stories have appeared in *Hobart*, *PANK*, and *Monkeybicycle*. He lives in Portland, Oregon with his girlfriend and daughter.

CPSIA information can be obtained at www.ICGtesting.com
Printed in the USA
BVOW04s1714270515

402100BV00004B/72/P

9 781621 051831